MW01172762

Paperback ISBN: 978-1-7372433-7-3

Hardback ISBN: 978-1-7372433-8-0

Blind Trust

Book One of The Trust Series

A.F. Presson

Plantation House
PUBLISHING, LLC

*This book is dedicated to my biggest
supporter, my husband Brian.*

*My Mom, who shares my love for
fiction, and my sister, who doesn't, but
makes an exception for me.*

The village at my back, especially Janis and Brenda.

This one is for you.

1

MAY 26, 2020

Death was chasing me. A dark shadow I couldn't escape. Strong and merciless, the ocean pulled at my body, refusing to let me go. I clawed at the black water as it slipped through my fingers.

Swim harder.

My arms and legs cramped from the struggle against angry waves, but I forced myself to push forward. A crack of thunder echoed in the storm clouds, while hard rain pelted the side of my face. In the distance, I looked back at the boat swaying back and forth, and a light skimmed over the swells of water . . . They were searching for me.

Let the ocean have you; it's better than being on that boat.

Saltwater thrashed against me, and I couldn't seem to get a breath. My eyes stung, and my lungs burned. Every time I made it to the surface, another wave knocked me under. I had to fight harder.

Don't let them see you.

My head throbbed, and my vision blurred.

Don't let them catch you.

There was no way I was going to make it. I couldn't focus

enough to figure out what to do as my mind tore between the will to keep fighting and the need to let go. A gravelly voice shouted from the vessel, the voice I would've known anywhere, and something dark told me they were closing in.

All at once, a strong and unrelenting arm wrapped around me and pulled me in the opposite direction of the current. Panic coursed through me at the thought of being captured, but my mind struggled to stay awake. Held tight against a hard, muscular body, I surrendered completely, collapsing from exhaustion, and everything went black.

My back hit a hard surface, and the jolt caused me to stir. Clouds swung to my left, then my right, rocked by the sway of the vessel. Back and forth, I drifted in and out of consciousness. A moment of terror ran through me at the thought of being back on that boat. His boat. The fear of what was planned for me caused vomit to rise up my throat.

I will not survive this.

I forced myself up on my elbows as panic overwhelmed me. Then, I heard an unfamiliar man's voice above me.

"You're okay. You can trust me."

* * *

May 28, 2020

I BLINKED PAINFULLY against bright sunlight from the window. Grogginess kept me from thinking straight as I pushed the blankets back and fought the urge to fall back asleep. My head throbbed, and I struggled to swallow, trying to wet my parched throat. My tongue swept across dry, cracked lips.

What happened to me?

Suddenly, the suffocating fear of the ocean returned, and panic seized my body. The crack of thunder and heavy rain . . . then what? Did the boat sink? How could I not remember? My stomach turned as I recalled the mouthfuls of saltwater, and my thighs were sore from my fight against the brutal sea. I thought for sure I would die. Did I?

No. No, I'm alive.

I took a few minutes to breathe in and out, and my lungs expanded with the knowledge that I breathed in air, not saltwater. The sun's warmth radiated through the windows, and my body relaxed. A door creaked, and I forced myself to wake enough to take in my surroundings. The large room had a sizable bamboo fan blowing a light breeze over my face. The feathery soft bed molded around my body.

Slowly and awkwardly, I pushed up on my elbows to get a better view. Overlooking the sea, the bright, uncluttered room was adorned with dark wooden beams on the ceiling and white furniture throughout. The sun shone brightly into the open, and airy space.

Beautiful.

A spirited voice came from the doorway, "I'm so happy you're awake. I hoped you would be!"

An older woman dressed in black walked into the room, holding a tray. Laying it on the end of the bed, she made her way to me. She fidgeted with the sheet, the lamp and anything else she could get her hands on. I couldn't help but notice her feisty nature. She had beautiful exotic features, even at her age, and a soothing bird-like voice that captured my attention immediately. Her gray hair had been pulled tight into a severe bun, and her posture rigid.

"I've been so worried about you, dear," she said. "You've been out for over two days."

Two days? How could that be? I recalled thinking I would drown, but then what? I tried to concentrate on the last thing

I remembered, but everything seemed so distorted. Someone else was with me, right? Yes. A man pulled me on a boat. He saved my life. . .

"How are you feeling? Oh, I can't imagine what you've gone through. I'll call Dr. Carlos for you. I know he'll want to see you now that you're awake." She fluttered around the room, leaving no room for argument.

"Oh. Well, thank y. . ." I tried to respond, but she continued as though no one else existed.

Is there an off button?

"The ocean's a brutal thing. We have tourists drown every year around the island. Of course, most have been drinking and carrying on something awful." She continued to find things around the bedside table to relocate, and then moved them back to where they were. "No respect for the sea. Not that I'm talking about you, dear, of course not." She patted me on the shoulder reassuringly. "Now, what can I do to help?"

Her head tilted to the side, and I waited to make sure she actually wanted an answer. When her eyes widened expectantly, I said, "I think I'm okay, just sore." My scratchy throat made speaking difficult. Stabbing pain shot through my head as I pushed myself up in the bed. I winced at the discomfort.

"Careful, you might pull your stitches. William said you had a nasty head injury when they found you." She hummed to herself as she fluffed the pillows behind my back and sorted the tray of food.

"I'm sorry, who is William?" I asked. A confused expression crossed her face.

Am I supposed to know these people?

"Don't you remember?"

Her question baffled me, and my mind hazed with confusion and shock. I racked my brain for information, but I could only remember the crushing fear of drowning and the relief of being rescued. My hands shook, and my heart pounded against my chest.

"I'm not . . . um. I can't remember. . ." I stared across the room without seeing anything in front of me. What happened? I couldn't even remember my name. My mind went blank as if someone had erased everything, and the thought terrified me.

What should I do?

I couldn't just lie there. There had to be someone I could call. I pushed at my mind and pulled at memories that weren't there. Every time I focused, a sharp pain shot through my skull. Where was my family? Friends? Why had I woken up alone?

Concern crossed her kind face at my distress, but she covered her unease with encouragement. With a calm demeanor, she leaned in to embrace me. Of course she's calm. She knew who she was.

"Now, don't you worry. This is probably perfectly normal after what you've been through. My name is Isabel. I'll call Dr. Carlos, and he'll take care of everything. He arrived back in town last night." She made her way to the door.

"Can you tell me where I am?"

"Of course. You're on San Adler Island."

San Adler? The unfamiliar words did very little to comfort my distress.

Isabel scowled at my plate. "What are you waiting for? You remember how to feed yourself, right?" She hurried through the door without another word.

The smell of breakfast hung in the air, but I wasn't confident I could eat. My stomach felt nauseous, and my head ached, but I'd never get my strength back if I didn't try. She had packed the tray with fruit, eggs, and bacon, and brought a large glass of water and a mug of hot coffee that smelled heavenly. My throat felt painfully dry, so I tried the water first. I took small sips in fear of rejecting it, and the cold crisp water helped soothe the dry ache. Even though my body needed water, I craved the coffee. I pushed the sugar to the side and added the sweet cream to the mug. I didn't have to think about it.

Sigh. If everything were that easy.

After a few more sips, exhaustion took over. The caffeine was no match for what I had been through. I pushed the tray to the other side of the bed and collapsed on my fluffy pillow. As tired as I felt, swirling emotions and anxiety kept my mind from getting the rest it needed. *Relax? No.* My mind wandered to things like the material of the sheets, shade of the wall, or how Isabel got her hair that tight. I couldn't wrap my mind around any of it; the traumatic experience, or her hair, and I had a difficult time believing it wasn't a bad dream.

Unsure what my next move should be, I laid in bed, contemplating my situation. I wasn't convinced I could walk out of there, and I definitely was in no shape to be on my own anyway. My eyelids were heavy, and my body gave in. "You can trust me." I remembered that voice vividly as it echoed throughout my head. My mind eventually gave up, and I slowly closed my eyes.

* * *

THE BLAST of a ship's horn woke me, and I stretched my rigid muscles. I wasn't sure how long I'd slept, but I could tell the food and rest had made a difference. Isabel must have stopped by while I slept, because the tray had disappeared, and the curtains were pulled closed. I hoped it was Isabel. The thought of someone else coming in gave me the creeps.

I contemplated trying to walk. Even though I felt strong enough to make my way to the bathroom, I doubted my balance. I swung my legs over the side of the bed and stood to test my strength. I trembled, but my feet were steady. I hoped the door across the room would be the bathroom, so I took baby steps in that direction.

The spacious area had a huge walk-in closet and tile shower, decorated in all white tile and the same rustic wood accents that were in the bedroom. The place had a spa-like atmosphere with the light colors, and a plush rug that tickled my toes. The towels were as lush as the bathrobe hanging on the door. A bag of new clothes sat on the counter with toothpaste, shampoo, and soap on the sink. There laid a note from Isabel:

These are for you, dear.
Please make yourself at home and
Dr. Carlos will stop by in a little while.
Love, Isabel

A giant clawfoot tub in the corner caught my eye, and I said a silent thank you to whoever designed it. That vast cast-iron haven gave the coffee some competition. I turned the water as hot as I could stand it; I needed to feel clean.

Unease settled over me as I realized someone changed my clothes while I was unconscious. A large t-shirt hung below my knees and draped off my narrow shoulders. I pulled the shirt slowly over my head and observed the bruised and tender spots on my scalp, back, and arms. Black rings circled my wrists, and a bruise that looked to be a handprint wrapped around my upper arm. What happened to me?

Dried blood caked around the stitches on my scalp, and the area felt swollen and sensitive. Washing my hair would be difficult. More bruises ran down my forearm and shoulder, but I hoped they would begin to fade in a matter of days. The marks around my wrist indicated struggle and a fresh wave of anxiety washed up my throat, as my hands covered my mouth to keep from crying out. I couldn't remember anything, and I wondered if my mind protected me from something dark.

Push through. You're safe now.

My head lowered over the sink, building up the courage to look in the mirror at a face I might not recognize. Nervousness consumed me as my pulse pounded and my muscles tightened. I pushed my fear to the back of my mind.

Stop being a coward.

Slowly, I lifted my head and my breath left my body when I saw an absolute stranger. I'm not sure what I expected. It wasn't that I was disappointed in the person staring back at me, because she wasn't unattractive. Maybe heartbreak for the memories I knew deep down I'd lost. There were mixed feelings coming face to face with those unfamiliar features; distressed that I was unacquainted with the person I saw.

I leaned forward, bracing myself on the counter, and my long dark hair fell forward across my shoulders. Even pale, my cheekbones stood prominent. My lips felt raw, and an angry split pulled at the corner of my mouth. Bruises across my cheek and dark circles under my eyes showed my exhaustion. I had to be in my late twenties, at least. Not old, but not a teenager either.

"Who are you?" I searched for any feature in the mirror that I would recognize. If only I could have remembered something meaningful, something personal. Frustration welled up within me, and before I knew it, my fists started beating against the hard glass. Angry tears ran down the bridge of my nose, and the healing split in my lip pulled apart. It took all the energy I had to vent the panic within, but it had to happen. A tiny crack in the mirror pulled me from my meltdown, and my gaze drifted to the break, such a likeness of myself. My shaking fingers traced the small split in the glass until something in my reflection captured my attention.

Dark brown eyes stared back at me, and the panic subsided. The only thing that gave me comfort since I'd woken up were those eyes. I'm not sure why, but a sense of calm washed over me. A familiarity that I couldn't explain. But, even that didn't stop the tears from running down my cheeks. I was a hot mess, and hated the sight of the fragile person staring back.

That is not who you are.

I didn't know who I was. Taking a deep breath, I turned away from the stranger in the mirror. One shaky leg at a time, I stepped into the warm bath and felt my body absorb the heat. After carefully washing my hair, I drained the red-stained water, then refilled the tub again. A calm surrounded me, and I felt somewhat human.

There was security in that moment, and I wondered how long I could stay in the tub before Isabel checked on me. My hosts seemed decent enough, but being in a strange place after almost dying in the ocean had me on edge. I hid out until the water turned cold and forced me to move.

The clothes that Isabel left were ideal; soft leggings and a light, stretchy tank that fit perfectly. I needed comfort right then. Combing my hair around the stitches took some time and effort, but I finally unsnarled the tangles. Leaving it to air dry, I walked back into the bedroom; if nothing else, I must have been more pleasant to look at.

Thank goodness. That was gruesome. The inside would take more time.

An older Hispanic man stood gazing out the window. He turned, smiling when he heard me enter and put his arm out to shake my hand. I stood in shock for a few seconds at the sight of a strange man in my bedroom. He tried his best to alleviate my obvious discomfort. "I'm Dr. Carlos. Did they tell you I was coming?"

"Yes, Isabel did." I shook his hand.

He motioned for me to sit. Dr. Carlos had a warm kindness in his eyes that calmed my initial anxiety. Although an older man, he was handsome. His dark skin tone and thin gray hair created a striking combination.

"I hope you don't mind that Isabel let me in. We're very laid back here, considering we've known each other for years." I did mind, actually. When I didn't respond, he continued, "Well, I heard you had a head injury, so I tried to come as soon as possible. I'm sorry that work had me out of town when they brought you in. Mr. Reed offered to fly me in that night, but I couldn't leave my post. Let me take a look at William's stitching skills."

"William?" Isabel mentioned the name earlier.

"Yes, William is the captain of the boat that rescued you, and married to the fiery Isabel. Lord knows she's a handful, am I right?" he said, chuckling. "Isabel says William stitched your head laceration." He stood over me while inspecting my scalp for swelling. "Stitches are healing well. I may have to put him on my payroll." I sat blank-faced as he chuckled at his own joke. I struggled to find any of it funny.

"Anyway, we'll give you a couple of weeks to heal before taking the stitches out. I'd like to prescribe some antibiotics so we can prevent an infection. The ocean can be a nasty place to get an injury." He watched me for a moment to make sure I had absorbed his instructions. Then he moved to sit in front of me. "So, Isabel tells me you woke with some confusion. Tell me, Sophia, what do you remember?"

My head jerked up.

"Sophia? Who is Sophia?" My heart squeezed, and breathing became difficult. My body had an unusual reaction to something so unfamiliar.

"Well, you are. That's what we assumed, anyway. The necklace you were wearing had Sophia engraved on it. Do you not remember who you are?"

Pulse-pounding, unease crept its way under my skin. I needed to calm down before I had an anxiety attack. *Am I prone to those? Who the hell knows?*

"No, I can't remember. I keep trying, but it's like hitting a wall," I said with defeat. "I only recall the thunder overhead and someone rescuing me from drowning. That's bad, isn't it?"

Dr. Carlos studied me quietly for a few seconds, then replaced the concerned expression with a kind, reassuring smile. His poker face was almost as perfected as Isabel's.

Well, try not to worry. As you heal, your memories have an excellent chance of returning. This can be common when someone goes through this much trauma. But, in the meantime, get some rest and let me know if something changes, okay? I'm here if you need anything." With a gentle smile, Dr. Carlos left and assured me he'd be back the following day.

What was I supposed to do until then? I stared around the room and considered my options. Swimming was definitely out. Boat ride? Yeah, right. I couldn't spend the next twenty-four hours eating, napping, and bathing. But then again, people paid good money for that type of vacation.

A sizeable cozy armchair in the corner of the room caught my attention, and I curled up there with my knees bent against my chest. I'm not sure how long I sat in front of the window. It could have been minutes or even hours. Boats sped by, and the white crests of waves broke into foam. Although the view was remarkable, I stared as though the answers to my problems were washing ashore.

Concentrate on what you do know.

Sophia . . . The name sounded foreign and familiar at the same time; a comfort that nagged at me.

Who were these people taking care of me? Were they wealthy? Did they want me to leave? I didn't know where I'd go if they did. I felt so lost, yet grateful; it was a complicated feeling to process.

The thought weighed on me that I should've been doing something; calling someone. Dr. Carlos wanted me to focus on healing, but I needed to find out where I'd come from. How would I do that? A voice in the back of my mind shouted to be careful.

You don't even know these people.

The residence had a private dock, and several boats were secured alongside. Every now and then, someone would stop by delivering boxes and packages to the house, and I considered asking them for a lift. But, where? *"Excuse me, sir, can you give me a ride? I have no idea where I'm going."* Brilliant idea.

It was official. Staying in that room would drive me crazy. I couldn't make it one day. The itch to escape was too great. I looked around the room for a television or phone but didn't see either one. It made me wonder if they even had internet access on the island. An eeriness rolled through me at the thought of not being able to contact the police or emergency services if I needed it. But, they did seem more than hospitable.

Curiosity pulled my attention toward the door. It didn't appear to be locked. The thought of fresh air sounded lovely, but I didn't want to seem like some creepy lost girl walking around the property either. Isabel didn't say I had to stay in my room, and a quick stroll wouldn't hurt anything. Right? I mean, how much trouble could I get in?

2

I prayed the doorknob wouldn't squeak as I turned it. My feet took small steps down the long hallway, while I kept an eye out for anyone nearby. I realized I probably looked like a psychiatric patient escaping an institution.

You're a guest here. Quit being ridiculous.

I straightened my spine and walked down the hall with my head held high. The hardwood floors creaked from age; I could never sneak up on anyone in this place.

Every room was bright and airy, similar to mine. Large paintings adorned the walls, and the rustic light fixtures appeared to be a hundred years old. Several rooms were off the same hallway as mine, and I casually wondered how the staff kept from getting lost. Loud voices and clanging metal sounded from the corner, and I went on a mission to find out more about my hosts.

Eventually, I ran into the hustle and bustle of a large kitchen. Enormous stone walls and flooring were the first things that caught my eye. Wall-to-wall stainless steel appliances took up the room's extent, and various silver and copper pots hung from the ceiling. A hint of apple baked in the oven and the ripe smell of vine tomatoes hung in the air. A robust woman chopped fresh herbs that smelled like rosemary.

How did I know that?

A small wooden table holding wildflowers sat in front of a window, where a couple of women wearing black uniforms and aprons were sipping coffee, probably taking a break after preparing breakfast. Isabel stood at the counter along with several other women, and it seemed as though they were preparing for the next meal.

"Oh, Sophia! I'm so happy to see you up and about," Isabel exclaimed. She wiped her hands on her apron and smiled. "Can I get you anything? Margaret, our chef, just prepared the most amazing apple tarts if you're hungry."

Margaret stood by the stove with a sullen expression. Her excitement over the apple tarts seemed somewhat lacking.

"No, thank you. I thought it might be nice to go for a walk." Everyone in the kitchen stopped in his or her tracks, and they stared at me curiously.

So much for staying under the radar.

"I didn't mean to interrupt, please excuse me," I said as I backed out of the kitchen.

"Nonsense. Our gardener will take you for a tour of his flowers if you'd like. They are a sight to behold, and I believe he's all caught up this morning." Isabel offered.

"Oh, that's so sweet, but I wouldn't want to impose." I hoped she would take the hint so I could explore alone. Everyone just kept staring like I had two heads. How could I think with everyone hovering?

Isabel smiled. "It's no bother at all, Ian loves showing off his hard work. Plus, we don't want you to get lost. This place is large, and the area is unfamiliar." Isabel continued to smile. It was remarkable how she could give an order but made it sound like a suggestion.

The woman is talented.

A young man walked through the back door shirtless. He didn't look tall, maybe average. At first glance, I would've guessed he was in his mid-twenties, but something told me he appeared older than he was. Anyone could tell he worked outside by the gold of his skin and the definition in his arms. Dark blonde hair had been kept short, and his eyes were bright blue; handsome, for sure. But, he had a guarded expression as he stared at me. He observed me just like the kitchen staff. Looking back, I should have seen the signs of intelligence and awareness in his eyes.

"Ah! Ian! We were just talking about you." Isabel walked over and put her arm around me. "This is our Sophia. She hoped to see the stunning flowers we told her about and maybe take a walk. Would you be so kind as to escort her?"

"Really, I don't need a chaperone. I'll just take a quick stroll and be right back."

Isabel's face stopped me in my tracks.

"I'm sorry, Sophia, Alex will never allow it," Isabel said. "We promised we'd watch over you until he returns from his trip."

"Mr. Reed might change his mind if he knows Ian is escorting her. . ." murmured a staff member by the sink.

Isabel gave her a stern look, then turned toward me with a beaming smile. "Now, off you go, enjoy the sun and get some fresh air."

Ian offered his arm and led me out the same door he entered. The clenched jaw and tight smile told me he agreed to be polite. I was certain this wasn't on his list of things to do after he got off from work. But, the need to get outside overpowered any thoughts of being a burden to him. I breathed in the fresh salty air, and the sunshine warmed my cold frame of mind.

The house was much bigger than I anticipated; at least

three stories tall, on top of a small cliff, but it could have been more. The exterior had been composed of stone and white stucco, and the old tile roof gave it a clean tropical look. An ancient cobblestone pathway took us around the back of the house to a manicured green lawn. The grass stopped around sixty feet out from the house, and the gardens took over from there. Flowers surrounded the property, and the shorter arrangements were placed along the backside of the house, so the ocean view hadn't been obstructed. It was perfect.

Everything had been stacked and strategically planted everywhere. Snapdragons, lilies, roses, and tulips lined the garden, and by far the most beautiful assortment of flowers that I'd ever remembered seeing. *Ha!* I had to chuckle at my own private joke. Did I even remember seeing a garden before?

Ian's brow furrowed and a look of concern crossed his face as he watched me amuse myself. "You don't like it?"

"No! It's stunning. I just told myself a joke."

His head turned to the side, probably worried about my sanity.

"You've placed everything so perfectly. The colors and design are flawless. And snapdragons can be so finicky," I continued.

"You know about flowers?" He looked intrigued.

"I'm honestly, not sure. It seems familiar, but I don't know why."

He studied my features while I focused on the gardens. I tried to ignore him, but his eyes burned into me, as hot as the sun. It didn't feel inappropriate, more like his attempt to figure me out. Like I was some kind of puzzle for him to solve. I tried to think of something to say; I hated the awkwardness. Especially since he still had his shirt off.

He does like to show off his hard work. Isabel said so herself.

"How long have you worked here?"

"Five years."

"Have you always had a passion for gardening?"

"Not really. I took over my father's responsibilities to make him proud. He's worked for this family his entire life until Mr. Reed asked him to retire to enjoy what time he has left."

"Mr. Reed sounds like a good man."

Ian's jaw clenched and his lips pulled tight.

"Yes. Mr. Reed was a good man. Then his son took over."

I didn't ask him to elaborate. I assumed something in his past had left a bad taste in his mouth. I made the smart decision to change the subject and avoid asking questions about the Reeds.

Ian had a youthful appearance about him, but there was an old soul that lived under those massive muscles and cocky grin. His kind, but guarded personality came across as if he'd been through a lot for his age. His eyes seemed younger than mine, but not by much.

"So, Ian, tell me more about yourself."

"What would you like to know?"

"Everything. I have time to waste and nothing to keep my mind occupied."

Ian turned out to be a talker. Much more than I anticipated, but this was a good thing, considering I didn't have much to share. I guessed he needed to warm up to someone first.

He walked around with me for over an hour and kept the conversation light. It was comfortable, relaxed, and exactly what I needed. The gardens were his pride and joy, just like his father's. Something told me he didn't keep them this pristine for the Reeds. Ian did this for himself because he truly did love it. He came across as though this job made his father happy, but I sensed a deep satisfaction in his work.

Back behind the flowers, a hidden cobblestone path led to a private herb garden. I didn't understand the feeling at the time, but excitement bubbled up in me at the thought. As we came into the clearing, I saw rows and rows of herbs, green and fragrant. The trees created a privacy barrier around the plants, so one really had to be searching for the garden to find it.

"Some of these are precious commodities on the island, due to our lack of resources." Ian tried to be a useful guide, educating me about each one, but I didn't need him to. I immediately kneeled beside one in particular and took a long green stem from the plant. He watched as I inhaled the citrus scent and smiled.

"I've always loved lemon thyme." I looked up at Ian, surprised. "I'm not sure how I knew that," I admitted.

"Maybe your memories are coming back."

"I really hope so." The thought lightened my mood instantly, and I stood to walk around the garden. Over by the tree line, a small path carved into the curtain of forest and then disappeared.

"Where does that go?" I asked.

"Nowhere in particular. The path heads down into the forest for miles. It's a beautiful hike if you get bored one day."

"Thanks. I might just do that."

"Let's get you back before Isabel starts hunting for us," he suggested. This disappointed me, but I knew he was right. That woman was like a general. I'm sure he could tell by my gloomy expression that I had no desire to go back to my room. "I'll stop by this week if you'd like, and we can do this again."

"That gives me something to look forward to," I said with gratitude. Ian escorted me back to my room and leaned down to kiss my hand before he left. As he pulled away, I noticed an appreciation in his eyes that wasn't there earlier. I wasn't sure how to respond. He had been so kind, and I felt grateful for the time he spent with me, but I didn't think that attraction was there for me. I mostly felt sorry for him. Sorry for the obvious pain he had experienced.

After Ian left, I went into the bathroom to wash up and more products had been left for me on the counter. Another note from Isabel said Mr. Reed purchased some new clothes, and they were hanging in my closet. I had to figure out my next move, so I wasn't relying on his kindness, but the thought terrified me.

As I left the bathroom, there stood a thin, young woman setting a tray on my bed. "Hello," I called out. "You didn't have to bring it all the way here. I could have come to the kitchen to eat."

Her clothes were too big, and without any curves, they hung off her shoulders and made her look even more petite than she was. She couldn't be more than sixteen or seventeen years old. Bashfully, she kept her head down, so her shoulder-length dark hair hid her face, and she refused to make eye contact when she spoke. She was a beautiful girl, but she wasn't aware of it.

"No ma'am, it's no trouble at all. The dining room isn't typically used when Mr. Reed is out of town, so we thought you'd be more comfortable here."

"Oh, I see. I'm told my name is Sophia. It's very nice to meet you."

She couldn't hold back the small grin and whispered, "I'm Mary."

I couldn't get over this tiny mouse of a girl, and I was intrigued by her timid personality. She seemed a bit old to be this shy, and I yearned to know more about her.

"Well, Mary, please come back to visit anytime, I don't have anyone to talk to, so I'd appreciate the company."

Mary smiled again, and her posture relaxed. She gave a

small nod and left as quietly as she came. Something about the girl made me want to wrap my arms around her. Protect her from harm. She reminded me of someone, and the memory was so close to the surface, it tormented me.

My dinner was delicious. The cook had prepared a variety of fresh white fish and veggies that were seasoned to perfection. After dinner, I found a collection of romance and mystery novels on the nightstand and spent the evening getting lost in someone else's world. As much as I enjoyed the book, it also brought a hint of depression. I needed to know my own story.

The night wore on, and I decided to turn in. It was so black outside; I could barely make out the lights that shone from the dock. A dark hazy figure caught my attention by the boats, and chills ran up my arms. The dark figure paused, staring directly at me. Waves of madness rolled all the way to the window, and I'd never imagined so much animosity from a single shadow. A chiming clock pulled my attention over toward the wall. I glanced again through the window, but the dock was empty.

Get a grip. You're safe here.

I changed out of my clothes and concluded I'd sleep better without pajamas. The air was too muggy for me to rest comfortably, and I wasn't leaving my window open. I kept my panties and tank top on and laid over the pillow-top comforter; the light breeze from the overhead fan blowing across my skin. I didn't have a chance to replay the baffling day, because sleep claimed me instantly.

At some point during the night, I became restless. I tossed and turned in my sleep with visions of pitch-black waves crashing around me. The fear of something greater came toward me, and my mind fought to determine my greater enemy. Drown, or face something more terrifying. What could be more horrible than drowning?

A voice echoed in my head to wake up. *Wake up.*

I blinked in the darkness after rousing with the ominous feeling that someone stood in the room. Watching me. A shadow of a man leaned against the chair with his arms crossed in front of him. I sat up immediately and turned on the bedside lamp, but the figure had disappeared. Did I imagine that? I laid back down, knowing I would lose my mind over paranoia, but sleep refused to take me. What did it mean?

It doesn't mean anything, go back to sleep.

But, something inside me doubted the truth of it.

A small knock at the door startled me. After I woke in the middle of the night, it took a couple of hours to relax. But, when my mind finally relented, I slept peacefully. I opened the door and found Mary standing on the other side with her head down.

"I'm so sorry to wake you, ma'am, but Dr. Carlos is here to check in."

"Thanks, Mary. I'll only be a few minutes."

She left to deliver my message, making her escape as if knocking on my door had made her nervous. I made my way into the bathroom to brush my teeth and make myself presentable. My hair had dried in pretty waves down my back, so I brushed it out to remove the tangles and devoted extra time around my stitches. My face had more color that morning, and the dark circles were fading.

The clothes inside my closet were over the top. I had everything from undergarments to casual and eveningwear. If Mr. Reed expected something in return from me, he would be sorely disappointed. I panicked at the thought, but my choices were to wear the new ones or stay in the same clothes I had on. A gray cotton romper seemed innocent enough, so I pulled it from the hanger and slipped it on.

About the time I walked back into the bedroom, another knock sounded at the door.

I plastered a smile on my face to greet Dr. Carlos. "Good morning Dr. . ." My breath caught, and my heart skipped. Sweat beaded on the back of my neck, and I couldn't seem to force my mind into functioning properly. Blood rushed to my face. When did I become a thirteen-year-old girl?

"Good morning, Sophia. I'm Alex Reed. I wanted to introduce myself and see if you needed anything." That voice. I remembered that voice.

Taller than average, Mr. Reed had dark wavy hair and beautiful olive coloring. This guy was way too attractive for his own good. That voice, he was the one who saved my life that night. I had so many questions for him, but I wasn't sure where to start. Coming face to face with my hero had been exactly what I'd wanted. What I wasn't prepared for was acting like a mute.

When I didn't speak, he continued. "I'm sorry I haven't been to see you sooner, I had important business to take care of." I stood frozen like some kind of crazy person staring.

Speak Sophia. Please say something.

"Are you alright?"

"You saved my life. I remember you."

"Is that all you remember?" He grinned. He probably thought I'd lost it.

I shook my head to clear the seductive fog that surrounded me. I finally stopped staring and acted like a grown woman. "I'm sorry, this is all so strange. Would you like to come in?"

Mr. Reed hesitantly stepped into the doorway but refrained from walking in as if he didn't want to impose. "Please don't apologize. You've been through a lot. You don't have any idea how you ended up in the water that night?"

"No, but I'm hoping my memories will start coming

back." We locked eyes and stood in the room, staring at each other. I had hoped there would be more information from him about that night. I searched his eyes for answers he didn't seem to have, and I could only imagine he looked in mine for the same. I wasn't sure how long we stood there before Dr. Carlos walked up behind Mr. Reed.

"Sophia! So happy to see you up and well. Are you ready for our appointment?"

"I'll leave you to Dr. Carlos," Mr. Reed offered. "But I'd love to take you to lunch if you're up for it."

I glanced at the clock on the wall. It was almost noon. I really had slept in. "Yes, I would like that."

"Me too."

Standing there with eyes locked for several seconds, we ignored everything around us. Dr. Carlos eventually cleared his throat. Alex nodded his appreciation to the doctor before leaving.

After Mr. Reed departed, I turned to find the doctor quite amused. "So, are you ready to get started?" I asked.

"Whenever you are." He grinned as he came into the room.

Why is he grinning at me?

He asked more of the same questions from yesterday, but unfortunately, I didn't have any new answers. My injuries were healing as expected, and he made me promise to get some rest.

"I know you're getting restless, but don't let your anxiousness put you in harm's way. Laying around is the best thing for you right now, Sophia." He assured me that he would be back in a few days to follow up as he headed out the door.

I freshened up before lunch, then spent the next half hour reading by the open window. Mr. Reed was pleasant.

Okay, pleasant to look at.

But, considering I had amnesia, I knew that I had to be careful. Until my memories came back, I didn't trust my judgment about anyone. Mary stopped by my room to let me know Mr. Reed would be back soon, and would take me outside to meet him. It felt a little awkward to be summoned for lunch. Why didn't he just stop by my room and escort me down himself? On second thought, I would have a few minutes outside to myself, and the idea brought a smile to my face.

3

Mary directed me toward the lawn under a massive tree beside the gardens. Long, willow-like limbs of the tree blew out toward the water and did little against the midday sun. There was an unbeliev-able view of the flowers and ocean from there. Across the trees to the side, the top of straw huts emerged that could have been a local village or market.

Fishing boats lined the docks, and people moved like busy ants working together toward a common cause. It was quite entertaining and I could see why he chose that spot. A size-able handmade quilt and a picnic basket waited underneath the tree.

Someone's trying to flatter you.

"You can wait here for Mr. Reed. He shouldn't be long," Mary said quietly. Then, she trotted toward the house as fast as her feet could carry her. I would have loved to know what went through that girl's head.

The thick blanket acted as a decent barrier to the hard ground. But, boredom kicked in, and I laid back to soak it all up. The heat from the sun soothed me, the air smelled salty, and for the first time in days, I just let myself enjoy the moment.

"Well, you look comfortable," a masculine voice rumbled.

I opened my eyes to see Ian standing over me, amused.

"I know how you feel about my flowers, but having lunch with them is moving a little too fast. That's like a gardener's second base."

He appeared light and carefree. The guard obviously lowered since our last encounter.

"You're funny, aren't you?" I grinned, enjoying the banter. "I'm waiting for Mr. Reed." At those words, an irritated smirk replaced the grin, but he quickly covered it with a smile.

"If I had a woman as beautiful as you waiting for me, nothing would keep me from being here," he said with certainty.

I didn't know what to say. Was Ian flirting with me? There might have been just a little bit more sparkle to his smile that day, more twinkle throughout his eyes.

Proceed with caution, but be considerate.

"Are you on a break? You're welcome to sit down."

"Sure, I'll keep you company for a few minutes."

Ian sat beside me and began educating me about the island. I asked him about the locals, fishing, and the sites I needed to see. He patiently answered each one and went into detail about the most beautiful beaches to visit.

"The fisherman's village is a good place to pass the time. When I was younger, I would sit out there for hours watching the boats come in with their daily catch."

He had a fondness for the island when he talked about it. The locals were part of his family.

"I would love to take you to some of my favorite spots," he offered. He stared at me for an uncomfortable amount of time before snapping out of it. "So, have you had any luck with your memory? I'm sure it's hard not knowing where you came from."

I shook my head slightly while staring at the ocean. Defeat must have passed over my face, because he quickly spoke again.

"Don't stress. I'm sure if you give it time, it will all come back. And, we'll all be here for you when it does."

I smiled, hoping he knew his words had calmed my anxiety. A few minutes or so passed when a shadow of someone hovered over me.

"Enjoying yourself, Ian?" Mr. Reed asked.

"Hi, boss. I'm keeping our guest company since someone left her all alone. And, you know what you always say, 'What's mine is yours. . .' Isn't that right?"

This is an entirely different side of Ian. One, I'm not sure I like.

"I don't believe that's what I was referring to. And, I'm sure you have things you need to be doing." Mr. Reed stared at Ian as if he would throw him over the cliff if he didn't move in the next three seconds.

But Ian was cocky. He slowly stood, smiling the entire time, then sauntered off toward the house; but not before he turned around with mischief in his eyes.

Uh oh.

"Sophia, maybe we can go on one of our walks later if you're up for it. When the sun goes down? I had a wonderful time with you yesterday." He smiled as he turned to leave.

He would be trouble. I could feel it. Mr. Reed's eyes burned holes through me, but I couldn't figure out what I'd done. The man was intimidating. "Is there a reason you're angry with me?"

He blinked as his head jerked back. "I'm not angry with you."

"Really? So you always look like you're ready to pummel someone?"

He cracked a grin and finally took a seat beside me. "I don't do well when people get in the way of something I want."

"So, you're a man who always gets what he wants?"

"Always," he said, trying not to smile.

"And you just happen to want that seat, correct?" I teased. He was much more attractive when he relaxed. The need for total control and world domination vanished, and the real man underneath remained.

"Something like that, yes."

"Well, Mr. Reed, it's all yours now."

"Yes. Yes, it is." He pinned me with a calculative glare. *Better watch this one, he's good.* "Please call me Alex."

"Alex, I would love to hear more about you."

"What would you like to know? I'm afraid there isn't anything too exciting to tell. I'm a pretty boring guy. Mostly all work and no play."

"Tell me everything. If I can't remember my life, I'll relish hearing about yours."

Alex did not disappoint. He told me that his father started a pharmaceutical company, and did business all over the world. His main facility was on the island, not only because it was cost-efficient, but also offered the villagers an income. A softness crossed his face when he referred to the locals, and it made him even more appealing.

Control yourself.

His father had passed away a couple of years ago, and everything had been willed to him. I couldn't imagine the pressure of running a large corporation.

"Is this what you always wanted? To take over for your father?"

"Not necessarily. I'm not sure what else I would've done. My father groomed me for this position since I was young, so I've never had an opportunity to think about other options."

Alex didn't know how fortunate he was to have a past, to be able to talk about it. The thought caused a deep ache in my chest for my history. My family.

"So, what's my next move? Is there someone I can reach out to? Someone must know where I came from."

"An emergency call was made to all the islands in our area in case someone called in a missing person's report. So far, no one has responded."

My stomach clenched from disappointment. Was I not loved at all? Didn't anyone care? What a horrible person I must have been to be abandoned entirely. I sat deep in thought when I glanced up to see Alex staring at me.

"Hey, I have to be honest with you. I'm glad you're still here."

"Thank you, Alex. But, I can't keep relying on you for support. You've done enough for me, and there's no way I can ever repay you."

"Sophia, it's only been a few days. Give yourself some time to heal, then I'll help you figure out your next step. There's no need to rush anything."

There was something very alpha-like about his nature. A strong dominance radiated from him, but a tender side as well. Right now, he was gentle because he feared I was fragile.

You're not fragile. He just doesn't know it yet.

"How old are you?"

"Thirty-four," he answered.

"How old do you think I am?"

"Late twenties maybe," he guessed. "Tell me about yourself, Sophia, or what you know."

"But, I don't know anything."

"Sure, you do. Any favorite foods so far?"

"Ooh, probably the fish. It tasted divine."

He chuckled. "That's a good start. At least I know you like seafood. What about hobbies?"

Does he mean besides being shut in my room without anyone to talk to? Maybe I should keep that to myself.

I didn't want to seem ungrateful. "I enjoyed walking around the gardens, and I love to read."

"Read?"

"Yes, I've been going through the books that Isabel left on my nightstand. There's a lovely romance with just a hint of danger that keeps my mind occupied. I'm absorbed in it right now. If I can't remember my own story, I'll get lost in someone else's."

He stared at me in deep thought, and I couldn't determine if it was appreciation in his eyes or just curiosity. I wish I knew what went on inside of his head.

"You have the most beautiful brown eyes I've ever seen," he said.

Well, that wasn't what I expected him to say. I started to speak when I heard someone call out.

"Alex!" exclaimed Isabel from the house. "I'm so sorry to interrupt. I completely forgot the wine you asked for." She apologized over and over while quickly walking toward us.

She better be careful, or a hair will fall out of place.

"No worries, Isabel. We haven't eaten lunch yet," he reassured her while never breaking eye contact with me. He knew just as well as I did that she used the wine excuse to be nosey. His smile said it all.

He discarded the suit coat and rolled up his sleeves, looking more young and carefree than I had seen him. We had a light lunch of cheese, fruits, assorted meats, and wine. Afterward, we took a leisurely walk. He showed me more of the property than I saw yesterday, and the thought crossed my mind he made the extra effort to show up Ian. A competitive nature existed between those two, and it wasn't something I wanted to be in the middle of.

We walked to my room, and he kissed my cheek goodbye. I stood there for several seconds when he acted as though he would say more, but he opened his mouth to speak, then took a couple of steps backward as if he didn't trust himself.

"I'm sure we'll see each other this evening." He disappeared without another word.

It baffled me how calm, collected, and talkative he could be one minute and cold as ice the next. I took in my quiet and solitary chamber. It was going to be a long day.

The evening came and went; the only person that walked through my bedroom door was Mary with dinner. I tried to chat with her again, but it was no use. That girl shut down like a vault and departed as quickly as she came. The loneliness was miserable, and I went to bed early to end the torturous night. I might have been a little pouty that Alex didn't come back that evening as he'd said. I enjoyed the laid back lunch we had earlier, chatting over wine and cheese. But, I was ashamed to admit my clinginess was probably a direct result of my desperation to have someone to talk to.

I laid in bed, contemplating what I wanted. Like, really wanted. What if my memories didn't come back? What if I had to start over on this island and make a new life for myself? Would that have been so bad? I had to stop waiting on things to happen for me and be proactive. So the next day, I had a plan. First, I would get out of that room and explore. And I would do it on my own.

* * *

THE NEXT MORNING, I got dressed and prepared for my private adventure. Any decent explorer knew you couldn't start out the door without a cup of coffee. So, I waited until breakfast arrived before I began my day. I knotted my hair on top of my head and grabbed some comfortable shoes.

Considering my wannabe sugar daddy supplied me with multiple pairs.

Quietly, I opened the door and stuck my head out to see if anyone was in the hall. Sneaking out unseen would add to the overall rebellious vibe I had set for myself. Chattering echoed down the long hallway from the staff, but their voices sounded distant. I headed in the opposite direction of the kitchen.

Like a ninja, in my mind at least, I crept down a long hallway of doors but eventually found myself sneaking toward what appeared to be a laundry room. Some staff members yelled in a language I couldn't understand, and seemed oblivious to me. One robust lady had a snarl on her face that told me she would be the last person I'd want to upset. The other gentleman, frail and skinny, chased behind her while he hung on her every word. It was quite comical to watch.

As they walked out with baskets of clothing, I snuck in behind them and found a screen door to the side of the dryer. Bingo. I walked out the door unnoticed, and it gave me a boost of confidence. Totally ninja. And what if they did see me? I'm not sure what I had been worried about. I wasn't a prisoner, and what were they going to do? Ground me?

You don't know what they'll do. You don't know these people.

I walked over to where Ian revealed his hidden trail and started down that path in the trees. He told me it could be followed for hours, which sounded ideal for what I had in mind for the day. It was a bright and sunny morning, and having the sun on my face lifted my spirits.

The herb garden came into view, and I knew I was on the right track. The small trail wound toward the garden and into the cluster of thick green forest. That was the route I searched for. I pushed back thick vines and took my first step into the lush, but somewhat creepy woods. Greenery hung everywhere and vines wrapped from tree to tree. Large colorful birds watched me as if they sensed I didn't belong. The random thought entered my head to watch for snakes, but I ignored the possibility. That wasn't something I wanted to think about.

Sure, I'm confident that will keep them away.

The trail overgrew in some areas, but not enough to conceal the path. I wasn't sure how long I had walked, but finally came into a clearing with a rippling stream that flowed across my path. Water trickled down into a small pool, then continued back into the forest. In the silence of the day, the stream echoed around the trees and demanded attention. It seemed like a good time to take a breather, so I found the perfect spot on a large moss-covered rock situated between the trees and water. For a moment, I forgot where I was, entranced by the graceful flow of water as it caressed over the top of each stone. I filled my lungs with air and released it slowly.

This is what I needed.

My back straightened as a shadow hovered beside me. Someone watched me.

Undoubtedly, your ninja skills would have picked up on someone following you.

My head turned to find a sloth hanging on an old heavy branch. It startled me at first, but when I realized how unhurried it was, I could only giggle. Then the giggling turned into a full belly laugh with eyes watering. I had to admit, sloths were kind of cute.

Sure, just sit out in the middle of nowhere, laughing like a psychopath.

I composed myself and proceeded with my self-discovery hike. As slow as sloths were, it still made me uncomfortable that he gawked at me like that. After another hour or two of walking, shrill voices captured my attention. The squeal of a child resonated through the trees, and a high-pitch laugh followed. Pushing limbs and weeds aside, I stepped out of the forest into a small village with maybe ten to twelve man-made shacks. Most of the roofs were thin and sparse, and the straw that remained, hung black and weepy and provided little shelter. In the center was a large fire pit, and I assumed they used it for cooking.

This place looked run-down, and the thought crossed my mind that Alex could do something to help them. This wasn't at all what I had imagined when he told me about the locals. Women and children in scraps of clothing played outside while worn-down men pulled weeds in the garden and cleaned fish. Swollen bellies and sunken eyes indicated they were all malnourished.

This is heart-breaking.

Curious heads turned toward me at the sound of my footsteps. Everything around me froze for a few seconds, but it felt like minutes. As soon as they noticed me, they took off into their huts, yelling a language I wasn't familiar with.

A horrible surge of panic ran up my spine, and I decided to stay perfectly still. Something told me not to run, but nerves kept me from moving anyway. Several thin, angry-looking men came out with guns to confront the stranger that trespassed on their land and disrupted their families. One guy, in particular, a scrawny man with a snarled face walked toward me aggressively and pointed his gun in front of my face. My gaze dropped toward the barrel of the weapon as he shouted something over and over I couldn't comprehend.

If I had ever learned a second language, now is a good time for those memories to come back. . .

"I'm sorry, I don't understand!" I screamed. "I wasn't

trying to intrude, I mean no harm!" He searched me for a weapon. Then, grabbed my bruised upper arm and drug me to the largest hut toward the back of the village. I considered screaming for help, but had a feeling my plea would not be heard this far away.

He flung me forward, and my bare knees scraped against the uneven dirt floor. While he continued to yell, all I could think about is how Isabel wouldn't allow me to go alone that day. At that moment. I understood.

I woke in an unknown land, I had no experience with these people, and I refused to listen to anyone. I wanted what I wanted and damn the consequences.

I guess you'll learn to listen, Sophia. Is this what it takes? Does a rusty gun shoved in your face make things clearer for you?

The cheerful chap moved in front of my face and yanked my hair back so he could look me in the eye. My stitches screamed against his grasp. He got close enough that his foul-smelling breath hit me in the face, and I had to breathe through my mouth so I didn't gag. He quietly uttered something to his friend, and they both began to chuckle. My stomach turned when the greasy smile revealed black decaying teeth. He circled me like a shark would circle its prey and glared with unapologetic eyes.

As he stopped in front of me, he forced my chin up toward his face, and I jerked away from his grasp. He reached back to hit me across the face, and I yelled out the only thing I could think of at that moment, "Reed." The word gave him pause, and he glanced over at the other captor.

"I'm a guest of Mr. Reed," I tried again.

He stepped back, considering my words. Disgruntlement covered his face, and he turned his head to spit at the ground. He pointed at the other man and nodded his head toward the entrance of the tent. The second man left, and the first stayed on me with the gun. I deflated slightly and hoped those words saved my life. If I made it out of there, I would never pretend to be a rebel again.

I wasn't sure how long I had been there, but I hoped they hurried because he seemed impatient and bored. He paced back and forth as if contemplating what to do with me. He didn't want me there. An untrustworthy intruder imposed on his territory and his patience had run out. He stepped forward and placed the gun's tip under my chin, putting pressure on my skin. He was telling me if I moved, he'd kill me and I didn't need a translator to comprehend that. He ran the barrel of the gun down my neck to my chest, and the click of the hammer resonated inside the tent.

His slimy smile made my throat close up, and sweat broke out across my brow. His intentions were clear. I had to figure out a way out of that hell, and I needed to do it quickly.

He stepped forward and squeezed the sides of my face hard with his other hand. My cheeks hurt from his grip, and I cried out more from fear than pain. He moved down in front of my face, mumbling something else I couldn't comprehend.

You should probably be thankful you can't understand him.

At that moment, sunlight hit the inside of the tent, and the captor was thrown off me. Alex stood there, breathing hard, angrier than I had ever imagined him being.

Without a word, he picked me up and took me from the hut. I shook all over, and my grip around his neck had to be uncomfortable. He started to sit me on the passenger side of the jeep but thought better of it. Alex walked around to the driver's side as I continued to cling to his neck. I couldn't let go just yet and he must've sensed it.

Yeah, you're a ninja, alright.

When we arrived back at the house, over half of the staff waited for us. Isabel wrung her hands from worry, and Ian glared at Alex. He carried me right past the crowd, never sparing them a glance. They must have sensed his anger because they gave him a wide berth. A few of them shuffled behind us, and I wasn't certain they should. We arrived in my bedroom, and my nerves were shot, mainly because of Alex's rage. He opened the door, turned and shut it in Isabel's face without a word. He laid me gently on the bed and stepped away as if he needed distance between us.

I sat on the bed and watched as he stood tense in front of the window without seeing anything in front of him. Alex's fury vibrated throughout the room. Could he be that terrifying? Yes, but he would never hurt me. I'm not sure how I knew that, but I did. I gave him a few minutes to breathe and regain his composure before I spoke. "Alex."

"Don't," he demanded sharply. "I don't want to hear it."

"Are you not going to let me explain what happened?"

"Do you have any idea what could have happened out there today?" he asked. "Do you know what they do to intruders like you? Do you?" His shout rang out across the room, and I jumped.

"Stop yelling at me!" We stared at each other and tried to breathe through the thick fog of anger. I took a few breaths and tried to speak without sounding like a crazy woman. "Please . . . stop yelling."

His shoulders dropped, and his rage defused.

"Look, I know I messed up. Trust me, that occurred to me the moment the gun pointed at my face."

"Sophia, for the sake of my temper, we may want to skip the specifics right now."

I nodded a couple of times, knowing that sounded like smart advice.

"I'm sorry. I know I shouldn't have gone by myself. But who would have gone with me? Do you have any idea how incredibly lonely it is to not have anyone after losing the last twenty to thirty years of your life? I see Mary only at mealtimes, an occasional visit from you, Dr. Carlos . . . I'm trapped in this room, with no memories in a strange place, and I have nothing! I feel like Rapunzel . . . and I'm not even blonde!" Tears began to fall down my cheeks, and I realized I had ruined my chance of not coming across crazy.

Smooth.

Strong arms wrapped around me, holding me tight while I finished my breakdown. I had quieted to the occasional sniffle when he said, "I like brunettes anyway."

We both chuckled, mostly out of relief that it was over.

"Please, Sophia. We are not trying to trap you, but we do want to protect you. I want to protect you. But that is only going to work if you let me."

"Thank you for coming after me." My comment went without a reply, but his sigh told me he heard me.

He took a deep breath, then stepped back to speak, "I'm sorry. I wasn't aware how isolated you've felt since you arrived. I haven't been the host you deserve."

"I'm not trying to be ungrateful. I really do appreciate all you've done for me."

Alex stared at me, contemplating something, but I'm not sure what.

"Would you like to have dinner together in your room tonight?" he asked. "Just you and I?"

"That sounds great. I'm not ready to be alone."

Alex nodded and gave me a half-smile. He had some food sent up to the room while I showered. After I cleaned and bandaged my battered knees, we piled up on the bed to eat. Stories of a mischievous young Alex kept my mind occupied and thoroughly entertained.

It was after Alex left that the shadows hovered and the nightmares returned. And something deep down warned me the worst was yet to come.

4

The next day, Alex showed to have lunch with me on the beach, but said work had him busy that evening. A part of me was disappointed, but thankful he'd taken some time out of his day to make sure I wasn't alone. It meant more to me than Alex could have ever imagined.

After we ate, we walked along the white, sandy beach, and he taught me about the different villages in the area. The island didn't appear large, but was densely populated since the Reed family offered employment opportunities for the locals. The market would be the safest village on the island to explore, and where he preferred I visit if I felt the need to escape the house. The one I happened upon yesterday was by far the worst.

"They are criminals, Sophia. They take what they want and have no regard for authority. Not that we have any level of law enforcement on the island anyway. The ones we do have are no better than mall-security. But, a stranger coming into their village is nothing but a threat to their families.

They'd kill you rather than risk a chance of their families being harmed."

"Can they be helped? Surely if someone offered assistance. . ."

"I have. Many times, in fact. They're too stubborn and proud to accept help from an outsider. Although I grew up here, I'm American by birth, and they know it. They despise me for it."

"But, they seem to respect you. The only way I could stop him was to yell your name. He immediately halted."

"A few years back, an elder's wife got very ill. He grew desperate when he realized she would die. He showed up at the house on his knees, begging me to save her. We sent Dr. Carlos to treat her with antibiotics, and the infection eventually cleared. We've never spoken about it again, but I suspect that was their way of repaying me. I wouldn't expect them to do it again."

I considered everything Alex told me about the villagers. The island intrigued me, and I wanted to soak up as much as I could. I was excited to visit the market and the marina, but I wasn't sure I wanted to go alone after yesterday.

I tried to pass the evening by reading, but mainly thought about Alex. Something about him made me feel secure. It could be because he saved me that night, but I couldn't shake the feeling there could be more. If only I had a radio I could listen to or a television to watch, maybe I could think about something else. Isabel looked at me like I was crazy when I asked. Apparently, televisions in bedrooms were undignified. Mary brought dinner that evening and stalled after she laid it on the bed. She stood nervously with her hands clasped at her waist, and her words stuck in her throat.

"Mary, is everything all right?" It wasn't like her to hang around for long.

She raised her head, and tears filled her eyes. She opened her mouth to say something, but quickly closed it again.

"You know you don't have to be afraid of me, right? Please, talk to me if there's something on your mind."

"Oh, ma'am. I don't know what to say. I've never felt so ashamed," she cried.

"Sweet girl, what do you have to be ashamed of? I can't imagine you hurting a fly."

Tears streamed down her face. I walked over to join her on the bed. I grabbed her hand in mine and pleaded with her to talk to me.

"I saw you . . . I saw you the day you snuck out, and I didn't stop you."

I tried to find the words to comfort the guilt she felt. She thought she carried the blame, and she couldn't have been more wrong. I'm disappointed that my ninja skills were lacking, but more so that she was so distraught.

"I'm a grown woman, Mary. It wasn't your job to monitor me."

"But, I know this island, and I know what that village is capable of doing. I should have warned you. I just thought you needed some time to yourself, and I had done you a favor."

"Thank you for telling me. But, know that I would never hold you responsible for my ignorant actions. Next time, maybe you can come with me?"

Mary's brows lifted, surprised at my suggestion. "Well, yes, if you'd like."

"Mary, please don't ever be afraid to tell me what you think, okay?"

"Thank you, ma'am," she said quietly. "I have to be getting on with my day." She stood to leave, and I couldn't help but observe the intelligence and awareness in her eyes.

I ate dinner in the quiet and decided to have another bath

out of boredom. I soaked in hot water until my eyes were heavy, and I quickly dried off to search my glorious closet for something comfortable. I found a pink cotton nightgown that looked more like a long tank top. I slipped it on, and the super-soft fabric clung to my curves.

I guess you're getting used to the closet? Shut up.

I pulled my hair into a bun and retreated into the world of my novel. The story followed a young woman trapped by darkness, determined to free herself no matter the cost. Halfway through the story, a scrap of paper fell to the ground. As I picked it up and turned it over, the words struck me like a knife to my heart.

Like a bird that used to fly,
Trapped in a cage, left here to die.
Will I ever see the sun again?
Or will this darkness do me in?
LR

I studied the words written on the piece of paper and the sorrow the writer must have felt overwhelmed me. My gaze lingered on the handwriting. I held on to the paper to use as a bookmark. But, I kept thinking back to the words again and again.

A knock demolished my thoughts like a freight train. When I answered the door, Ian stood with a furrowed brow and concerned eyes.

"Hey, is everything alright? You haven't heard from the officers on my case, have you?" I asked.

"Oh no, I'm sorry, Sophia. I just wanted to stop by and check on you after what happened in the village. Is there anything I can do for you?"

"I'm fine, but thank you. It's sweet for you to stop by and check on me."

"This may be a little forward, but I just want you to know that you can come to me if you need anything. I, well, I like you a lot, and I'm here for you. That situation could have ended much worse, and if it had, I would have burned that village to the ground. Alex doesn't always make time for people outside of work, but I would have gone with you."

"Thank you, Ian. I'll remember that next time."

"Night, Soph."

Ian left, and I couldn't help but remember his face when Alex brought me back from the village. He blamed Alex. That's why he acted so angry. But I was the only one to blame for that little excursion.

I read for a little over an hour until something outside the window caught my attention. Someone swam in the ocean, and I could barely make out what appeared to be a man. The moonlight shone just enough to see his lines and curves on top of the gleaming water. It was a beautiful thing to watch, and it didn't take me long to recognize the physique.

Alex swam laps back and forth like it was a backyard swimming pool. I watched him for several minutes, unable to look away. It took me a bit to realize that he now stood on the beach, staring up at my window. I jerked back behind the curtain and prayed he didn't see me. When I peeked through the curtain split again, he'd disappeared.

My heart finally slowed to a reasonable rate when I heard a knock at the door. I spun at the sound, and my heart pounded once again. I cracked the door open, and Alex stood there in shorts. My mouth went dry, and I couldn't stop staring. This man took great pride in his body, and it showed in his cut abs and muscular arms. Would it be awkward if I ran my hand over his bicep? *Yes. Yes, it would.* Water dripped from his hair and ran down his chest. My appreciation was visible, and there wasn't anything I could do to redeem myself at that point.

"Alex, hi. What brings you by?" I had no idea what to say. My face flushed from embarrassment as the heat rose across my neck. Alex's gaze stayed awkwardly glued to the front of my nightgown. I had forgotten entirely about the thin material. I just crossed my arms in front of my chest and continued. "Alex, are you okay?"

"I um. I . . . " he stuttered.

"Do you need anything?"

"I just wanted to check in on you. I saw you standing at the window and. . ." Alex shifted from foot to foot and pushed his hand through his wet hair, agitated.

"And what?"

"And, I. Um, I worry about you."

"That's very sweet, but you've already done so much. Please don't feel like you have to worry about me. I know you try to spend time with me because I've been so lonely. And I do appreciate it, even if they are pity visits," I admitted, grinning.

Alex stood there for a minute, deep in thought as he chewed his bottom lip and ran his hand through his hair. "You have to know that isn't true. I don't know why, but you're more than that."

I lowered my head, uncomfortable, and speechless. Emotions I didn't expect ran through me and were difficult to absorb. I didn't know whether he scared or excited me. Maybe a little of both. "Well, thank you for checking in on me, but I do need to lie down."

He nodded while biting his lip and asked, "Would you like to spend some time with me tomorrow?"

"Sure, you know I would. But, I also don't want to keep you from anything important."

"You are important."

"You know what I mean, work, or something."

"I'll make plans and stop by in the morning to pick you up. Until tomorrow, Sophia." He smiled as he backed up to leave.

"See you tomorrow, Alex."

I woke at the sound of a rattle. The noise pulled me from a deep sleep, and I sat up on guard. I froze, thinking maybe I'd dreamt it. My heart pounded as moonlight shined through a split in the curtain and shed light on the turning doorknob. Someone had a key, and they were opening my door.

I jumped from the bed and tiptoed across the room into the bathroom. I couldn't decide what to do. I could scream, but I wasn't sure anyone would hear me. I knew I didn't have much time, and the urge to hide overpowered all other instincts.

I pulled the closet door open and stepped inside. Gently closing it back, I left a small crack to peek through. I stayed curled up at the bottom of my wardrobe, my breathing loud and shaky. My hands trembled as the bathroom door glided open, and someone shuffled in. As I cowered on the floor, large black boots were the only thing visible through the small crack. They stood still for several seconds before turning around and walking back into the bedroom.

Who would be coming into my room in the middle of the night? My imagination went wild at the possibilities. Could someone be after me? I wasn't even sure how to call for help if I needed it. I hated feeling paranoid, but life hadn't exactly been a cakewalk lately. Maybe they only had the wrong room. Sure, that was it. But, just in case, I decided to stay there a little longer. . .

* * *

May 25, 2020

THE AIRPORT DROVE ME INSANE. A collection of aggravated and impatient travelers forced together in massive chaos. I told my boss I'd probably have another delay in Miami, but there were no other options. Holidays were always the worst at airports, and Memorial Day was no different. People piled in chairs, trying to get some sleep, and luggage spilled over into the aisles. I needed to be home in my bed. I'd spent too much time on the road, and the two layovers I dealt with that day were not helping my mood.

I sat for a while, watching those around me. It seemed as though most of the travelers struggled the same way I did. I could tell by that man's downturned mouth, or how that woman stretched her neck, sore from sitting. Passengers were tense and ready to be home. Happy travelers did exist, and I wasn't going to lie; I fantasized about tripping them when they walked past me. It wasn't that I didn't want other people to be content, but my life was in an unhappy place, and their cheerful mood made mine escalate.

The growl of my stomach interrupted my thoughts of tripping giddy people. I should have found something to eat while I waited, but even though my body begged, I didn't have an appetite. I hadn't for days. I had been nibbling on fruit or snacks just to keep me going. The stress of work and family had run its course, and I wasn't sure how much longer I could last.

I loved my job, but it was time to change companies. My boss had gotten too demanding, too corporate. I missed the days of the small town bookstores that represented the local people. Now, it's all about rushing everything online to make sales. Not exactly what I wanted to keep doing. As far as publishing companies went, ours did very well. But I wanted to work with new talent and fresh ideas. I wanted the small town bookstores to thrive again. My restlessness had made me crabby.

You are in a mood, aren't you?

When I was younger, finding authors of books that fed the heart and soul intrigued me. Like hidden treasures that no one else had seen. Books that fueled a reader to change their life for the better and left them with a new outlook. Those were the days.

Novels were like chicken soup for the soul for me. No matter what I'd been through, I always felt like a book could take me out of my reality and into another. Someone else's job they loved or a family without issues. "You're acting dramatic again," I told myself. "It's not that bad."

A gentleman in front of me turned to see if I'd spoken to him. He glanced around, looking for anyone else besides me, then turned toward me like I'd lost my mind. "Sorry, sir. I'm just giving myself a pep talk." I responded awkwardly.

"Oh. Well, whatever works." he mumbled and turned around uncomfortably.

I needed a vacation. I hadn't taken a trip in so long, it was ridiculous. Maybe on an island with warm beaches and cold drinks. I could see if my co-worker Tina would like to go, or maybe Sophia. She would be all about that. I called her right then. To hell with this job and this airport.

* * *

Present Day

THE NEXT DAY, Alex showed up at my door, smiling with a cup of coffee. This man already knew that I needed my cup first thing in the morning. "Let's go gorgeous; we have lots to do."

"Where are we going?"

"You'll see," he said, smiling. He took my hand and led me out to a large garage with a selection of vehicles. "Choose one," he said.

"What?"

"Pick one you'd like to take today. Is there something here that attracts you?"

I turned my head purposefully toward him and grinned, "Yes, I believe there is."

"Careful," he warned, smirking.

I sauntered across the expanse of the garage and made a dramatic show of choosing. Alex stood to the side with his arms crossed in front of him, anticipating my choice.

"That one." I pointed to the sleek metallic gray BMW convertible at the end.

He dropped his head, and a chuckle echoed throughout the garage.

"What?"

"You are very predictable," he said as he showed me the BMW key fob in his hand.

Predictable or not, I loved that car. The sun shone on the hood of the convertible and fresh air smelled of citrus as we took a long drive around the island. But, the stranger in my room last night weighed on my mind. I finally built the courage to talk to him about it while we were on the road. "Alex, does the staff know that I'm using that particular room?"

"I would think that's obvious by now. Why do you ask?"

"Well. . ."

His forehead wrinkled in concern at the tone of my voice. "Sophia, talk to me."

"Someone came into my room in the middle of the night, and it frightened me."

"Someone who? What did they look like?"

"I couldn't see their face, because. . . Well, because I hid. In my closet." I threw my hands over my face in embarrassment. He would think I had lost my mind.

"Let me get this straight. Someone unlocked your door, came into your room in the middle of the night and scared you, but you think you have something to be ashamed of? Sophia, if someone came into my room like that, I'd be pissed. I'll question the staff about it as soon as we get back. You have my word. I'll also get Isabel to have the locks changed, okay?"

"I appreciate it, Alex."

We drove for several hours, the wind blowing my hair from side to side. I loved that car. Now and then, Alex sped up just to see the smile widen across my face. We reached an uninhabited side of the island, not one building or structure in sight. Grassy hills and rocky cliffs made up most of the scenery, with an occasional wild horse running across the terrain. Several children ran in the grass beside the road and waved to us as we passed, playing in the fields.

We parked on the edge of a cliff, and Alex stepped out of the car. "I want to show you something." He motioned for me to follow. Slowly and carefully, he eased down the cliffside and held out his hand for me. "I'll help you, I promise."

I couldn't imagine the grimace on my face right then. I turned around to step down, and my foot slid against the sandy rock. Alex supported me at my back with steady hands. If he kept touching me like that, I might have kept sliding. *Behave.*

"Just watch where I put my feet, okay?"

Sure. Just look down while holding on for your life to watch him climb down easily.

I rolled my eyes, knowing he couldn't see me.

I couldn't be sure how long it usually took him to make it to the bottom, but I was sure it was quicker than the time it took me. I didn't think I had a fear of heights, but the recent near-death experience tended to make a girl nervous.

"Almost there, you're doing great."

Sure.

A loud thump startled me. I jerked my head around to make sure Alex hadn't fallen. No, he had jumped the rest of the way and stood below me like some superhero. I took a step down and . . . *Oh no.* There wasn't anything to step on.

"The cliffside ends there, Sophia. Just jump, and I'll catch you.

"Catch me?" I asked nervously.

"Yes, it doesn't hurt too bad." I heard the laughter in his voice. "It's only about ten feet, sweetheart. You can trust me."

He hasn't failed you yet.

I leaped toward Alex, and his arms wrapped around me to soften the landing. He stepped back on one foot to balance himself. "See? Nothing to it. Come on, you're going to love this."

We walked twenty to thirty feet and emerged in an area surrounded by rope on all sides. I took a peek to see what could've been so important, but there was nothing but sand. "What is this?"

"It's a sea turtle nest. Wildlife management roped it off so people will know to avoid the area."

"That's amazing! I would love to see them hatch!"

"It can be difficult to time. The eggs hatch at night and give little warning. I've only ever seen it once, but I'll never forget it."

We continued down the beach, and Alex showed me an area known for having the best seashells. Not just the small white delicate ones, but also the impressive pink conch shells that were rare to discover. It felt like a hidden secret, somewhere only the locals knew about. Everything appeared natural and untouched. We spent hours exploring, and he was right, I did love it there.

"Let's go ahead and climb up here. It's going to be easier than the side we came down. Especially since you are holding me responsible for protecting your conch shell." He blankly stared at me.

"Yes, you are a doll." I winked at him. But, he was right. Climbing up there did seem more manageable, and we were back in the car in no time.

On the way home, he pulled over on the side of the road by a broken-down food truck. "Do you think they need help?" I asked.

"Help?"

"You know, with their truck. I think they have a flat . . . or two."

"Sophia, we aren't here to assist them. We're here to eat." He grinned and got out of the car. "Aren't you hungry?" he asked.

I followed him to the truck, praying I'd had my tetanus shot. Rust covered the exterior, and two of the tires were flat. A small hand-written menu taped to the window displayed the day's specials.

"You'll never have fish tacos like these, trust me. Mama Brenda has the touch, and I have to eat here at least once a week."

"Okay, but I have to warn you. I'm not sure why, but I believe I could be a taco connoisseur," I answered earnestly.

Mama Brenda, a tiny woman with a sweet smile, handed me a paper plate with two fish tacos. Alongside the tacos, sat a cup of homemade salsa. She gave him a couple of beers, and we headed back to the car to eat.

"Well, what do you think?" Alex asked.

"This is amazing. I can't believe you haven't brought me here until now."

"I can't believe you wanted me to change their tires." He tried not to laugh, but he couldn't hold it in. I sat stoned-faced in the passenger seat waiting for him to compose himself. I had to admit, he charmed me with his laid-back nature. He typically kept it hidden from everyone.

We finished our lunch and made it back in time to get cleaned up and changed before dinner. I collapsed on top of the blankets, and the smooth pink shell on my nightstand captured my attention. I smiled before I realized it.

Alex ordered a new lock for my door the next day and assured me that only he and Isabel had a key. He never found out who came into the room that night, but I didn't expect anyone to admit to it.

The next few weeks were more of the same. We still hadn't heard anything about the missing person's report. Alex took his boat over to San Brilee Island to speak with the officers in person, but they still hadn't had anyone come forward. He promised he wouldn't stop trying. The more time that went by, the more hopelessness seeped in. Would I ever find out what happened? I just wanted to wake up one morning without questions or a looming fear that someone waited for me, watching me.

To keep my mind occupied, Alex showed up at my door every morning with coffee, ready for a new adventure. Then, I'd completely forget about the confusion in my life for just a little while. I didn't want to think about how much I'd started relying on him—how much I needed him from day to day.

I went to sleep every night knowing I'd wake up drenched with sweat and shaking. But, in the morning, Alex would be there to make everything better. I was depressed that my memories hadn't resurfaced, and the nightmares seemed to be getting worse. But, at least I had him.

Like most nights, I spent the entirety tossing and turning. Visions of dark crashing waves, swallowing large mouthfuls of saltwater, and a rocking boat haunted my dreams. Over and over, I fought the water. Only this time, a shadow stood in front of me. I couldn't figure out why I was frightened because it didn't seem threatening, but I was. Chills covered my arms from the fear. A tall man, slumped forward by the look of his frame, lingered. I couldn't make anything else out except a red toboggan. Right when he reached out to me, I woke up.

Sweat poured off of me, and my nightgown stuck to my skin. I took in loud gasps of air, trying to catch my breath. Nail imprints marked my palms, and I forced my fists to relax before I drew blood.

What happened to me? I felt so lost and alone at that moment. I had no idea if I had remembered something or if those crazy nightmares were meaningless. I thought about talking to Dr. Carlos but decided against it. Maybe my imagination got carried away again.

I jumped out of bed and took a quick shower to wash the sweat away. Standing under the hot spray helped me relax, and my heart returned to a regular rate. After drying off, I wasn't in the mood to style my hair, so I braided it down one side over my shoulder. It would soon be humid and hot, so I pulled some shorts from my closet with a loose summer top.

Alex told me yesterday he would be working, so I needed to have a plan to keep my mind occupied. I gathered my sandals, sunglasses, and a book because I planned to spend some time in the sun to recharge. That's what I needed, time out of this room.

A knock on the door interrupted my thoughts and I opened the door to find Alex, at ease, and way too handsome that early in the morning.

"Are you ready?" he asked while he handed me a cup of coffee.

The man showed up at my door, unannounced, with

coffee in hand. Who did he think he was? Who was I kidding? I would have gone anywhere with him for that coffee.

"Ready for what?" I questioned while reaching for the cup.

"We're going to spend the day together. I have a surprise for you."

A surprise for me? Well, this day seemed to be looking up. It usually did when it started with Alex first thing in the morning.

"You don't have to work today?" I asked, intrigued.

"You're more important," he smiled as though he knew what those words would do to me.

"Okay, Alex. I'll bite. Should I change, or is this okay?"

"That's perfect. But I want you to promise me one thing. If at any time you feel like you are uncomfortable or unsafe, I want you to tell me immediately." His surprise made me a little nervous, but I didn't want him to know that his words scared me. This was Alex, and he'd never hurt me. He had always taken care of me.

"Okay. I promise."

He grinned and reached his hand out for mine, "You're going to love this."

Alex carried a backpack of supplies as we strolled across the lush lawn. We walked to the back of the property, where stone steps descended the side of the small cliff. The remarkable view of the ocean continued for miles and the calm and peaceful water didn't look anything like it did in my nightmares. I shook off the eeriness and focused on the beauty of it.

We arrived at the bottom where the stone turned into sand, and that's when I saw it. Sweat trickled down the back of my neck, and my breathing picked up.

Today wouldn't be complete without a panic attack.

"Sophia, are you okay?" he asked.

I stopped walking. I tried to nod, but I was quite sure I looked like a bobblehead doll. My lead feet refused to move. I opened my mouth to object, but closed it quickly.

Alex walked over and tipped my chin up so he could see my eyes. "I've been worried this would be hard on you. If it's going to be too much, then we can change our plans for today," he offered.

I couldn't say no to that face; he had taken off work to make the day special. Getting on a boat could've been what I needed to heal. What if it helped me get past the fear and nightmares that haunted me? I had to be brave.

Coward.

"No, I need to do this," I said with determination in my voice.

He studied me for several seconds. "You're sure?"

Nope. "Yes," I answered, forcing a smile.

"I'll be with you the entire time. You know I'll jump in after you if anything were to happen."

"Yes, I believe you've proven yourself." I bit the side of my lip, trying not to smile.

We turned toward the dock, and Isabel walked toward us. That woman handled everything, and I'm not sure how she did it. She had probably been making the ordinary woman feel inadequate since the sixties. Or, at least the seventies.

"Hello, Alex! I've stocked the fridge and cabinets for you." She beamed.

"Excellent, I'll go store our things, and I'll be right back." Alex winked before heading that way.

"Is William our captain today?"

"Not today. William only sails the boat when Alex needs to work aboard the ship. From what I understand, Alex called and told everyone at work he'd be unavailable today. No interruptions. He wants to spend some alone time with you," she said, smiling. Then she made awkward eye contact while she kept a very sly grin on her face.

Lord, make it stop.

"Really?" I was somewhat uncomfortable by her knowing stare. I knew he'd taken off work, but I assumed he'd still be taking phone calls and answering emails.

"Plus, William and I haven't had an off day together in a

CHAPTER 5 | 57

while, so this will be nice." She blushed. "You two have a lovely time, and I'll see you tomorrow." She strolled toward the stone steps. "And Sophia? I'll expect the details tomorrow."

Oh, dear God.

Alex came back and held out his hand for mine. The wood creaked as we walked across the dock, and he stopped in front of a gleaming white sailboat. Boat was a bit of an understatement. "This doesn't look like your everyday boat. I think that's more like a yacht."

He chuckled. "No, I guess it doesn't. I do have a small yacht. That's what we were on when we found you." He then added, "I use it for longer trips."

"Longer trips? Where were you sailing from when you found me?"

"Miami. We have a company there, and I had to stay a few days to handle some things."

He watched me closely. I'm not sure if he paused for me to cry or run. "Have you ever been sailing?"

"I probably wouldn't know if I had." I tried not to smile.

"Oh, yeah, sorry. Well, I promise I'll handle you with care."

That grin doesn't suggest handling with care.

The boat had to be about thirty or forty feet. Sleek wood accents shone under the sun, and white sails fluttered as though they were anxious to get started. It had a classic, timeless style to it that wasn't flashy. Something special drew me in with that one.

"How old is this?"

"She's over fifty years old. I bought her at an auction in England a few years back, and it was love at first sight."

"Really . . . are you prone to that?" I peeked up at him smiling.

A half-grin adorned his face when he looked my way. "Only twice in my life."

I broke eye contact with him to keep from blushing. We stepped onto the boat, and I felt something I didn't expect . . . exhilaration. I never would've imagined I'd be this excited. Fear was a distant memory.

"What kind of wood is this?" I ran my hand down the smooth railing.

"Mahogany and Cedar throughout."

"Does she have a name?"

"No, she doesn't. William always says I'll know it when I hear it. It has to be something special and unique. Something that means a lot to me."

"He's been with you for a long time, hasn't he?"

"Who, William?" he asked. My silence encouraged him to continue. "Yes, he's more like a father to me. My own father never had much time for me. William taught me to drive, sail, and pick up women." He smiled at the memory. "Thankfully, he's good at sailing. The rest not so much."

I loved the sound of his laughter. Something real and carefree escaped him. The next few hours flew by sailing the seas while Alex taught me phrases that every good sailor should know. Starboard, port, bow, and several other terms that I couldn't retain. My love for sailing equaled relaxing on the deck, soaking in the sun, and listening to the waves while Alex did all of the work. That worked out great for me, and he didn't seem to mind. I assumed he was just content that I could enjoy it instead of being terrified.

It felt completely different than in my dreams. Daylight helped, the waves were calm, and I felt safe with Alex—it wasn't the horrific experience I had envisioned. I started to wonder if I was actually scared of the ocean itself or if something I didn't remember had me on edge. Either way, it thrilled me that I enjoyed it because Alex sailed with passion.

If he wanted to be out on the water, then I wanted to be with him.

He anchored the boat so we could eat lunch on the water. Isabel had stocked a variety of chicken salad and tuna fish sandwiches. After we ate, we laid around and finished off the bottle of wine.

"You're going to love the farmers market. There are tons of fresh vegetables, fruits, and hand-sewn clothing," Alex said. "Plus, I want to introduce you to some of the locals that I grew up around."

The market sounded perfect. And, it amazed me that he knew I would enjoy that type of thing.

"I would love that. And I love this. Thank you for today. Sailing was something I didn't even know I needed."

He didn't respond. As he leaned in toward me, anticipation crackled, and my belly clenched. He moved leisurely in case I wasn't ready. But, he knew. He knew I wouldn't stop him. He palmed the side of my face, and his stare fixed on my lips for several long seconds. My impatience almost caused me to move toward him, but my lack of confidence kept me from budging.

His hand slid into my hair as his lips softly brushed mine. I gripped his arm, his muscles clenching from restraint. So many emotions simmered to the surface when he kissed me. My heart said yes, but my mind still wavered. A war raged within me, and a voice demanded that I choose a side. But I didn't want to. Battling with my heart and my head exhausted me.

Despite my conflicting emotions, I kissed him back. The need for him felt so strong; I pulled Alex closer to encourage his lips. I wrapped my arms around his neck and gave myself over to him.

After a couple of minutes, he pulled back and stared at me, breathing hard. "I always knew it would be different with you, that it would be better. But that was even more than I expected."

He pulled back and ran his thumb over my bottom lip. He stared at me a few minutes before moving. Alex stood and pulled me up with him. "Come on, gorgeous, time for you to sail us back."

"Forgive me, but I just assumed you wanted us to survive this trip."

Has he lost his mind?

"You're cute when you're joking," he said, grinning.

"Oh, I'm not joking."

Thankfully for Alex, we made it back in one piece. We returned late in the evening, and the sun had painted the sky a deep blood-orange. At one point earlier, he asked about heading back for dinner, but I wanted to stay out a little longer, refusing to let our evening end.

I couldn't imagine having a better date. If that's what I could call it.

When we reached the dock, I broke out into a run toward the sand. Alex wasn't about to let me win, and I heard him take off in pursuit. Laughter made it challenging to keep my pace, and the pounding of our feet on the dock echoed throughout the empty beach. But something happened. The darkness, the sound of running feet on the wood of the pier . . . a sense of déjà vu came over me, and I lost my breath. Fear. Pure fear overwhelmed me, and it stopped me in my tracks.

Alex struggled to slow before the force of his body ran all over me, his arms wrapped around my waist, and he stumbled, balancing us, so we didn't fall to the ground.

"Hey, are you alright? I almost ran right over you."

"Yeah, I guess I'm just tired from today."

Don't say anything to make him think you've lost it. Things are going well.

"Come on, let's get you inside."

I couldn't shake the feeling that someone was watching me. I could sense it. Chills covered my arms, and I instinctively scanned all of my surroundings. I hated being so paranoid and afraid. Who wanted to live their life that way?

You have to snap out of this.

Glancing up toward the cliffs, I did a double-take. Ian stood to the side with his arms crossed in front of him. Wasn't he afraid Alex would see him? Anger vibrated from the air around him. His eyes met mine, as though he wanted me to see him there. I couldn't figure out why that was important to him, but it was. I'm sure jealousy guided his actions; he had made his intentions clear.

Alex must've detected the change, turning my body to face him, "Sophia, talk to me."

My gaze returned to the top of the cliff, and Ian had disappeared. I couldn't say anything to him. I didn't want to cause any problems with Ian's job. They had known each other for years, and I just showed up here. Plus, their relationship already seemed rocky. "Just skittish in the dark, I guess," I said.

Alex released my hand and put his arm across my shoulders. "Don't worry, you're safe with me." He quickly changed the subject, trying to take my mind off the darkness surrounding us.

"I would love to take you to the market soon if you're up for it. And, there's also a surprise that you need to see," he added.

"Another surprise?" I asked. "What did I do to deserve these surprises?"

"You deserve a lot more than I can give you, gorgeous. But, I promise I won't stop trying nonetheless."

His thoughtfulness caught me off guard, and I abruptly stopped at his words.

"Are you okay? I promise you have nothing to be afraid of. You're safe."

Of course, I was. Just speechless at his honesty. I didn't know how to respond to this man who gave so much of himself and asked for nothing in return. I wasn't sure why, but there was a deep dark part of me that said I had never had that. Like my heart had never experienced it before.

"Yes, I'm okay. I guess I'm just amazed at you sometimes. Ever since you saved my life that night, you've gone above and beyond for me. I have more than I can ever wear in my closet, a chef at my disposal, and you spend time with me when I know you have other things that need your attention. Let's be honest. You don't know me at all. I don't know me at all. This is very generous for someone you just met."

Alex cleared his throat. He shuffled his feet from side to side, trying to find the right words. His eyes met mine. His expression was stern and decisive, deciding to be straight with me.

"I think we both know you mean more to me than that."

Alex wasn't in his comfort zone right then, and it was difficult to tell me how he felt. "You have to know how much you get to me. I can't think straight when I'm not with you, I have no desire to be with other women, and I have a desperate need to take care of you. Because that's what you deserve.

You deserve a man to put you first and make sure you're happy and safe. I don't know how to explain it, but the first time I saw you, I knew you would be mine. There has never been a doubt in my mind, Sophia. All I can do now is show you how much you mean to me and hopefully prove to you that we found each other for a reason."

I couldn't argue that an undeniable pull existed. And, as hard as I tried, I couldn't explain the connection. A small part of me thought I clung to Alex because he rescued me. But, maybe that wasn't it. Perhaps I just couldn't admit that there might be more.

"Wow," I whispered. "I honestly didn't expect all of that."

Alex looked almost bashful, and it made him seem much younger. At that moment, the confident businessman was gone. He showed vulnerability and insecurity I didn't expect. I still couldn't believe how our kiss escalated quickly, which is why I hesitated with my feelings.

"I'm not trying to rush you. You've been through so much, and I can't imagine how confusing everything is right now. Just know I want to spend as much time with you as possible, and I'll wait as long as it takes for you to feel the same way about me."

Alex kissed my hand and walked with me to my room without another word. So many emotions were running rampant. We finally stood in front of my door after a ten-minute walk that felt like an hour. I started to say something to ease the awkwardness, but he placed his finger over my mouth.

"Sleep well. I'll see you tomorrow." Then he vanished.

How was I supposed to sleep? Lasting fear from the dock combined with the declaration from Alex had me reeling. So much doubt and frustration about my memories held me back from him. Any detail, big or small, could have made things less confusing. What if I had already found the love of my life, and he searched desperately for me? I hadn't seen a wedding band, so I guessed that answered that question. I thought about the necklace I wore that night. Folded clothes were stacked at the bottom of the closet; my necklace sat on top. I hadn't built the courage to pick it up yet. It was the necklace that Dr. Carlos described.

I stood over the small pile of possessions, the only ones I had. After hesitating long enough, I reached down to pick it up. A small gold chain attached to a round engraved gold plate had "Sophia" inscribed in elegant writing. I slowly placed the chain around my neck and fastened it. Something about it brought comfort, and I wished I had picked it up before then. I said a silent prayer for my memories to return and for the nightmares to subside.

* * *

May 25, 2020

FOUR HOURS. Four hours for one flight delay. This was ridiculous. I thought about renting a car and just driving. After an hour-long phone conversation with my boss, I was in no condition to drive anyway. I'd explained to her about my unhappiness, and she laughed. She thought I was joking. It took a while to make her understand that I was very serious.

My job did not fulfill me the way it once did. She agreed that I needed a vacation and ordered me to take a few weeks off; then, we would revisit the conversation. But, the phone call tore my nerves up. I had never been good with confrontation, and my hands were shaking before I even dialed her number.

Calling Sophia about the impromptu trip was the easy part. Of course, she was all for it. That is one of the many things I loved about her; all in no matter what we're doing. I finally decided that flying out of Miami would be more accessible if I wanted to go to the Caribbean, so I'd just wait at the airport until Sophia got here, and we would head out together. Drop everything and go. I'd never been spontaneous about anything, and I could only imagine the jokes I would have to endure when Sophia arrived. *You know she's right.*

While I waited, I decided to get a drink and check out the departures. A half-empty pub seemed the perfect place to waste a few hours. I still hadn't eaten, and suddenly my appetite made an appearance. After I ordered some fish tacos and a beer, I settled in to plan the next three weeks. There were so many places I wanted to see. Mexico, Brazil, Puerto Rico . . .

You should have gotten that wax.

Damn it. I had forgotten the wax appointment.

"Mind if I join you?" A deep voice rumbled.

A well-built man stood over my table, annoying me by the look of arrogance radiating from him. His beautiful eyes and cocky grin said he knew what my answer would be. He didn't.

"Actually, I'm waiting for someone," I answered.

He didn't look convinced. "I think we both know that isn't true." He pulled out a chair and sat down to face me.

Great. He apparently doesn't speak English.

"I am," I insisted. "And, I'm not really in the mood for company."

"You are a beautiful woman. Did you know that?" he asked.

I shifted uncomfortably in my seat. "Is that the best you can do?"

Without responding, he smiled and leaned closer as though I fascinated him.

"What can I help you with?" I asked.

He stared at me for a few long seconds then said, "I just want to kill time by having a drink. Will you have one with me? After that, I promise to be gone."

I need to lose this creep.

"Okay, one beer."

He got up to order himself a drink and to grab me another beer. One beer and this guy would be gone. It's not that he was hard on the eyes. He was handsome. I just wasn't in the right place to be talking to men. I honestly hadn't met one in quite a while that sparked an interest. But, one drink, and he would be gone. What could it hurt?

6

PRESENT DAY

Oh, dear heavenly father, I wasn't sure I'd make it through the day. It felt like we had been walking for hours, and Alex hadn't broken a sweat. I couldn't help but look at him up ahead, as he confidently hiked the path that had to lead to hell. I was sure of it. I bet if I weren't with him, he'd be running it. The trail wound back and forth as tree roots blocked every step.

As if they made bets on which one could trip me first. I almost stepped on a snake, but Alex appeared in an instant directing me safely around it, as he always did. I just hoped he could protect me from feral villagers. That concerned me more than anything.

It had been almost a week since the conversation about our relationship. We had fallen into a comfortable routine of just enjoying each other's company while sharing private kisses and flirty touches. Alex wasn't pushy, but he made sure I knew his intentions and where he stood.

When he told me we'd be going on a long hike that day, I had no idea it would be so treacherous. And it was hot. Not just warm. Hot as hell. My shirt stuck to my sports bra and my hair matted to my head.

You are so pretty right now.

"How much longer do you think? I mean, I'm keeping an eye out for the gates of hell to open up at any moment, but it hasn't happened yet," I added.

He chuckled and kept walking. Chuckled.

Damn him!

After a few more minutes of silent swagger, he turned and offered me his hand. "We're here."

I stepped up beside him and forgot my fatigue. The view was incredible; it took my breath away, and I couldn't find the words to speak.

"Sometimes when my father was home, I would come here to get away. He always seemed to be yelling, loud and angry, shouting about the food, the gardens, or his linens. The staff stayed tense, and I could sense it. So, I would make my way here and swim all day. It's a long hike, and that's why I liked it. But, I've never shared this with anyone before, and I wanted you to be the first."

It was beautiful before, but now it meant something. The waterfall had two levels that cascaded down into a lagoon. Tall trees and lush greenery surrounded the crystal clear water. I couldn't tell how deep the water went, but I could guarantee Alex already knew the answer.

"Alex, this place is magical. Thank you for bringing me here."

"I want you to know me, Sophia. This place is a big part of my childhood, and I had hoped you would love it as I do."

He turned, climbing across rocks to lead me to the opposite side. It only took me fifteen seconds to kick off my shoes, lose my shorts and shirt, and make my way down to the lagoon. I used my ninja skills because of the heat, and the rushing cold water sounded so refreshing. I still had my bra and panties on, so I didn't feel too self-conscious.

It has to be more attractive than your sweat covered clothing.

Splash!

Alex jerked around so fast you'd think he heard a gunshot.

"Sophia! Are you alright?" he asked, panicked. He had already taken his shoes off to come in after me.

"I'm perfect. Absolutely perfect."

"What do you think you're doing?"

"Just cooling off a bit. Would you like to join me?" I teased.

Alex took off his clothes slowly while keeping eye contact with me. Thankfully he left his briefs on. I tried not to watch, but that was impossible.

"If you know what's good for you, you'll stop looking at me like that," he said with seriousness. "A man can only take so much, and your current lack of clothing isn't helping anything."

He eased into the water while watching me with a definite hunger in his eyes. The eyes that right then reminded me of a predator, as he swam toward me. My muscles strained while treading water, and I was thankful when he placed his arms around me and pulled me against him. I wrapped my legs around his waist and let him hold me up. The crisp water felt magnificent on my sweaty skin. Cool on a hot balmy day.

Alex's gaze drifted down to the necklace I had worn. "I always want to ask how you're coping with everything, but then I decide if you want to talk about it, you'll let me know."

"I'd rather not discuss it if that's okay. Otherwise, the confusion just causes more anxiety."

"Of course."

"How deep is this anyway?"

"It's about fifteen feet toward the center. This is where I learned to swim." He chuckled at the memory. "I came up here angry one day and jumped in, not even thinking it might be over my head. I almost drowned until the movements clicked, and my body took over."

"That's horrible. You could've drowned."

Alex grinned at my concerned expression. "How did you know you could swim?"

"I honestly didn't think about it. I just jumped like it was as natural as walking."

Now that he mentioned it, I could have drowned. What if I didn't know how to swim? I barely remembered the fight in the ocean that night. There were so many things I did that were natural. I didn't even think before I acted.

"Come on, let me show you the waterfall."

We swam around for over an hour, exploring the lagoon and the hidden caves. Rough playing in the water turned into more flirting, which turned into more touching. Alex grabbed my waist as I swam toward the edge and turned me around to face him. My back pressed up against the cold hard rock, but I wasn't concerned about it. He pulled me into him aggressively, and my legs instinctually wrapped around his hips.

His mouth came down on mine, and it wasn't at all like our previous kiss. This was passion and hunger fueled by weeks of holding back. My arms immediately went around his neck, and my body melted against his. I'm not sure how long we had been like that until I noticed a change in the air. A darkness that wasn't there before. I pulled back and fidgeted nervously.

"What's wrong?"

"I don't know. I can't help but feel as though someone is watching us," I admitted.

Alex stood on the rock and scanned the area for several

minutes. The feeling disappeared instantly. In its place was an eerie quiet that was almost as alarming.

"There's a slim chance someone is out this far. Not saying it couldn't happen, though." He reached down for my hand and pulled me up on the rock. Leaning down once more, he lightly grazed his lips over mine. "Let's get to the market. We have lunch plans, and we don't want to be late."

"Is this going to be another four-hour hike?"

"Um, no. I took you the long route. We'll take the shortcut back," he grinned.

I hoped the smirk on my face and the narrowing of my eyes told him exactly how annoyed I felt. I kept my wet bra and panties on, knowing it would dry quickly in the hot sun, I stepped back into my clothes and we made our way back into the forest, leaving the serenity of the waterfall behind.

He was right. It only took us a couple of hours to get to the market. It was nothing like my first village experience, and I loved it. Outside of the fishermen's market, straw and bamboo huts sat in a clearing surrounded by palm trees. People were setting up everywhere selling fresh seafood, vegetables, and fruits that I'd love to try. Women were sewing and making dresses, blankets, and wraps. We passed multiple tables, making our way to the backside of the market, and everyone we encountered smiled and waved our way.

These were the locals I had heard about. The first village I discovered had nothing to do with these kind people. About fifty feet behind a small hut sat a wooden shack where a short older man stood outside, cleaning fish. He smiled when he noticed us.

"Sophia, this is Miguel. As a child, he took on the difficult task of keeping me out of trouble. I'm sure you can imagine what a chore that was," Alex said with affection. "He and his wife, Anna, cooked for me at least a couple of nights a week growing up. They are preparing my favorite meal for us today."

"It's so nice to meet you," I responded.

"Welcome, Sophia."

Miguel had a kind smile and invited me into the cozy shack. The overpowering smell of oregano and saffron flooded my nostrils. The entire hut smelled delicious. On the inside, we walked into a small common room used for relaxing and eating. The wooden door at the opposite end of the room must've led to a bedroom, and the kitchen connected to the common room, where we stood. Various types of lumber made up the structure of the home. They didn't have electricity. Instead, lanterns sat on wooden tables around the room. It was very modest, and I could see why Alex would like it there. The simplicity was vastly different from what he was used to.

An older woman with long braided gray hair cooked over a cast-iron pot and turned to greet us with enthusiasm. "Ah yes! Please come in!" she exclaimed. "I'm Anna, Miguel's wife. It's lovely to finally meet you." She stood with her hands clasped in front of her as if she couldn't contain her excitement. "Alex hasn't stopped talking about you."

Alex cleared his throat. "Okay Anna, that will do," he told her.

Miguel led us to an area with blankets and pillows arranged in a circle, and Anna had a variety of fish, pork, vegetables, rice, beans, and cabbage salad set up in the center.

"Have you eaten casado before, Sophia?" Miguel asked.

"If I have, I don't remember," I said, somewhat embarrassed.

"Oh, you poor dear. Alex told us about your accident. Miguel should have used his brain before his tongue." She smacked him on the back of the head and said something in a language I didn't understand.

"No, it's okay!" I reassured them. "I forget myself sometimes."

Oh, how true. I had gotten too comfortable there, acting as though that was my life when I had family, friends, and a home that hadn't gone away. The question remained, would I ever find out who they were, or where that was? Did I want to find out? What if I was miserable? What if I didn't have anyone? Something told me that wasn't true. A voice deep within me.

Alex showed me how to eat the prepared food and it was my favorite dish yet. The fish tasted buttery and tender while the cabbage salad gave the meal a crunch that took it to a new level. The flavors were vibrant, the meat was fresh, and there was something about us sitting together in this cozy hut, an intimacy that made me feel close to them.

Anna told me stories about Miguel teaching Alex to fish and hunt. We laughed over plates of mango sticky rice, and I learned more about Alex from those two than I had from anyone else. Those people helped raise him, and their love for him showed in the sentimental stories and adoring glances.

The glow of the sunset had dimmed when we said our goodbyes and promised to visit again soon. Alex led me out to a dock where a small speedboat waited for us.

"I thought it might be late when we left the market, so I had the boat sent here for us."

He always thought ahead. Always took care of me.

"I had a lovely night. Anna and Miguel seem like wonderful people."

"That, they are. I'm not sure what I would've done without them growing up."

We took the boat back, and Alex escorted me to my room. When we arrived at the door, he turned and kissed me lightly. "I hadn't planned on mentioning this honestly. I didn't want to put too much on you."

"What? What is it?"

"We always have an annual banquet at the house this time of year for my employees, and it's a week from Saturday. We hold a formal event, and a couple of hundred people show up. If that kind of thing is too much, it's no problem for you to relax in your room and I won't mention it again. If you would like to go, as my date, then I want you to know that would make me very happy."

He continued, "You don't have to answer tonight. Just think about it, and if you want to go, then I can get Isabel to help you with your wardrobe."

A banquet? That sounded like a very fancy event, and I wasn't sure I wanted to put myself in that situation. But, I'd be with Alex, and he wouldn't leave my side. If I didn't go, would he take someone else? The thought made the hair stand up on my arms.

"You know, I think I do want to go. I'll be okay as long as I'm with you."

Alex smiled and pulled me into him. He placed one hand on the side of my face and stared.

"I've never looked forward to one of these banquets before. Did you know that?" He didn't wait for me to answer. Placing his mouth over mine, he showed his gratitude for accepting the invitation. After a couple of minutes, I pulled him toward me and prayed he wouldn't stop. His palm skimmed up the back of my shirt, and his other hand gripped my hip. My back hit the doorframe and Alex's body pressed into mine.

"Excuse me, sir," Ian announced. "Isabel needs to verify some details with you for the banquet next week. She's been searching for you for quite some time."

Alex didn't glance his way. He just stared at me while saying, "I'll be right down."

Ian made eye contact with me and finally stomped off, leaving us alone again.

"Sorry about that. I'll let you get some rest, and I'll tell Isabel to set up a showing for some dresses."

"Thank you for today."

"I should be thanking you." He said before he walked away. I shut the door and walked to the bathroom to shower and change clothes. It had been a long day, but an enjoyable one. I only laid in bed for a few minutes before I drifted off to sleep.

MY NIGHTMARES typically started in the ocean, but not that night. I ran. I ran away from something terrifying, and fear crippled me. I tried to determine the location, maybe a boat or a dock. All I could figure out is that I shouldn't be there, and whoever was after me wasn't someone I wanted to be around. I felt him getting closer, so I pushed forward and ignored the strain my lungs and muscles were under. I had to get away. I had to get to Sophia. Was she in danger too? The thought caused bile to rise in my throat. I turned a sharp corner and ran right into a tall unforgiving body.

A faceless man chuckled sadistically as he said, "Now, where do you think you're goin?"

I SAT STRAIGHT UP in bed, gasping, and my heart hammered in my chest. A wave of nausea rolled through me, and I ran to the bathroom heaving from fear. After I emptied my stomach, I covered the back of my neck with a cold cloth and sank to the floor.

This nightmare felt different.

Also, I couldn't shake the panic attack I had at the dock with Alex. There wasn't a doubt in mind that all of this horror happened. And, if I wasn't Sophia, then who was I?

The all-consuming feeling of reaching her devastated me. But where was she? Who was she? I wrestled with the thought of telling Alex that Sophia isn't my name and the shocking details about the nightmare. But it was just a dream, right? *Don't say anything until you know for sure.*

We didn't have any proof I wasn't Sophia, and until I had something concrete, it was best to keep it to myself. There had to be a way for me to find out who I was. Every nightmare was a piece of the puzzle coming together, but it wasn't happening fast enough. I slowly made my way back to the bedroom to lie down, but the effort was pointless. There would not be any rest for me that night.

7

I t was early. I couldn't see the clock on the wall, but it was too damn early to be knocking on someone's door. Whoever was on the other side hopefully knew to have a cup of coffee waiting for me, because I'd get violent if they didn't.

I opened the door to Isabel smiling. Without saying a word, she handed me the coffee and watched as I took a sip. Isabel smiled when I glared at her over the top of the mug. She allowed me a couple more sips, and then finally spoke.

"Alex told me to give you this if I want you to cooperate with me today."

"Alex was right."

"Yes, well. We have a big day today and so much to do!"

"Exactly what are we doing?" It was too early for this much drama.

Processing information was difficult for me in the morning, especially since I hadn't been sleeping well. I hadn't had any more nightmares in the past week, but the last one stuck with me. I could think about it, and I'd break out in a sweat. I didn't rest well at night for fear of having another one.

"We have to get you ready for the banquet tonight, dear! I have someone bringing gowns for you to try on, and a stylist is coming to do your hair, makeup, and nails," she said while clapping.

The banquet. I had completely forgotten that it was Saturday. All it took was for Mr. Green Eyes to flash his perfect smile, and I was like, "Yes, I'd love to get dressed up and prance around in front of hundreds of strangers instead of staying in my quiet room to read." I hung my head in defeat. Another knock interrupted my pity party.

"Helga! I had no idea you were coming." Isabel exclaimed.

"Mr. Reed zaid to come be of zervice." Helga barely got her sentence out in English.

She had an accent so thick, I had to listen carefully to understand her. The woman that stepped in my room stood probably two or three inches taller than Alex, and their shoulders might have been evenly matched. I wasn't sure if those pants were supposed to be capris, or if she had trouble finding some an appropriate length.

Short curly red hair and freckles adorned her face, and large unyielding eyes burned holes through me. I wasn't going to lie. I was nervous.

You should be.

"Helga owns the Island Spa and is absolutely amazing. She will take good care of you." Isabel assured me as she made her way to the door. She stopped to whisper, "She was raised in Germany, and so her accent is a little thick." She patted me on the shoulder and left.

"Vhat first?" Helga asked.

"Oh, well. You're more experienced than I am Helga. I'm fine with anything."

"I vant to start vith the vax!" Helga exclaimed.

"I'm sorry, what?"

Did she come with a translator?

"The vax!"

I planned to murder Alex. Helga could tell by the confusion on my face that I had no idea what she was talking about. She held up a jar of something for me to read. "Oh! Wax!"

Oh no. This was going to be bad, I knew it.

"Take off clothez!"

"You know, I really think I'm okay in that department. I shaved my legs yesterday so we can skip that part," I pleaded.

"No skip! Dress show vay too much skin!" she yelled in her thick accent.

I walked to the bathroom and removed my clothes, grabbing the robe that hung on the back of the door so I didn't feel so naked. When I went back out, Helga had a table set up with towels, lotions, wax, and other items I didn't recognize. I laid down on my back and said a silent prayer for the agony to be quick. Helga opened my robe, and I was completely naked. She stood over me, eyeballing where she would torture me first.

"Now, I vax."

She started at my ankles and worked her way up to my thighs. She really was very good. The pain wasn't near as bad as I anticipated. Plus, she gave my legs a massage afterward with an aloe cooling gel. I could have gotten used to the pampering.

"Thank you, Helga, that wasn't bad at all."

"Very Good. Now I vax more."

Wax more? What did she plan to wax now? Helga slowly spread my knees apart and began inspecting how much wax she would need. I seriously thought I might die of embarrassment.

"You don't want man finding fuzzy kitty," she explained.

Oh, my dear God. Did she just say I had a fuzzy kitty? Did I mention I planned to murder Alex?

Helga waxed everything she said she would. Legs, bikini, armpits, face, you name it, and it was hairless. She rubbed me down with the aloe afterward and the tingling sensation cooled the burning skin. But it couldn't heal the emotional trauma I had endured.

Mary brought my lunch, and after I ate, the stylist arrived. Tall and willowy, with long blonde hair, Joy could have been a model. She was reserved, quiet, and sweet. Definitely a breath of fresh air that I so desperately needed that morning.

"I want to highlight your natural beauty, so we won't use too much, okay? We will mostly showcase the dark eyes," Joy explained. She didn't say another word until she finished a couple of hours later. The silence wasn't awkward; it relaxed me.

"You like?" she asked.

My skin glowed from the bronzer and my makeup, applied in neutrals, made my brown eyes stand out. Long dark lashes were curled to perfection, and my lips looked glossed and plump. I felt stunning. She pulled my hair over one shoulder in large curls and painted my nails a neutral shade. I still looked like me, only enhanced. I had a fear of being so made up that I didn't look like myself, but that wasn't the case at all.

"It's perfect," I told her. "You are amazing."

She smiled, and to my surprise, hugged me before she packed her things to leave.

Isabel stuck her head in the door to see if I was covered. "Sophia! You look so beautiful."

I inwardly cringed when she called me Sophia. Was I deceiving those kind people by not being honest with them about my name? But, if they didn't call me Sophia, what would they call me?

She came into the room, followed by a small man with a

tall rolling rack. He was so short I could barely see his head sticking up behind the cart. He came around the rack and stood there, studying me from head to toe for longer than necessary. I pulled the robe closer around me, uncomfortable.

The man's suit couldn't get any tighter; I honestly wasn't sure how he moved at all. Sparse, thin hair had been combed straight back, and his lips pursed tightly. He would have been comical if he weren't so intimidating.

"I'm Louis. You have the honor of my services," he announced.

That is all he said. He didn't even care who I was, and that was actually refreshing. He unzipped the cover to reveal eight to ten evening gowns hanging on the rack. They were all gorgeous, and they had to cost a fortune.

Picking up a red dress, he inspected it while stealing glances at me. "Nope, not it!" he shouted.

He chose a green one with a sickened look on his face. "Whoever put this dress on my rack is fired." He threw it on the floor.

The next dress was black, and he studied the detail for a long while. I peered over at Isabel because the silence turned awkward. Clutching her hands together, she smiled like a proud mother. Isabel enjoyed this. I couldn't say the same for myself.

"We try this!"

I jumped at Louis's voice. I didn't move immediately, and he yelled again, "Now! Try now!"

I grabbed the dress and turned away from him to drop my robe. I stepped into the fabric and pulled it up around my chest. Someone stepped behind me to zip the back, and I said a silent prayer hoping it was Isabel. The strapless dress ruched in the waist then ran to my left hip. The high slit came to my left thigh, and I silently thanked Helga for the wax. I turned around, and Louis studied me, trying to determine if he was happy with his choice. He smiled and walked toward me with purpose.

"You are lovely," he said. Then, he stuck his hand down the front of my dress and pulled my breasts higher into the cups, so I had more cleavage. "Now, you are beautiful and sexy," he explained.

I stood there in shock. Again. Who did these people think they were? Did they not have any respect at all? I turned to the corner of the room and looked at the dress in the mirror. I completely forgot about the pain of the wax or the man helping himself to my breasts. They were masters of their craft. I couldn't imagine looking more feminine or exquisite. The dress hugged all of my curves perfectly. I felt sexy but also classy.

"My work here is done," Louis stated, then started packing up his dresses to leave.

Isabel brought a pair of black strappy shoes and handed me a small turquoise box wrapped in white ribbon. "This is from Alex."

I carefully lifted the lid. Inside the box laid a beautiful teardrop diamond necklace. It would look gorgeous with the dress. Perfect, just like him. I couldn't imagine what all of this had cost him, but he probably didn't care. What had I done to deserve someone so thoughtful and kind?

"Isabel? Why does everyone seem so afraid of Alex? He has been nothing but sweet and gentle. I can't see him actually hurting anyone."

She chuckled lightly and nodded. "His father ran a very strict household and taught Alex to do the same. He doesn't allow himself to get close to any of the staff, besides William and me. It's what he is used to, I guess, dear. But, never think that's who he is. He has his mother's heart and his father's upbringing. He battles with it every day."

I said a quiet and emotional thank-you as Isabel helped me with the necklace clasp. Then she left me to my thoughts.

After a few finishing touches, a soft knock on the door caused me to jump, mainly because I knew exactly who it was. With one hand on the door and the other on the doorknob, I said a heartfelt prayer to not mess anything up that night. To be someone that Alex was proud to have at his side. I remembered the girl in the mirror in the black dress and reminded myself to stand up straight and confident. Opening the door, I started to say hello, but my words were stuck in my throat.

Incredible. There was no other way to describe him. Alex wore a black suit with a white shirt open at the neck. Sexy, but relaxed. He styled his hair in that messy way I loved. We just stared at each other. I wasn't sure what to say. *Yum.*

"Sophia, you . . . just wow."

"Thank you. And thank you for the necklace. I love it."

Alex stepped into the room and pulled me toward him. He ran his hand down my lower back and leaned down to softly kiss my shoulder, so he didn't destroy my makeup. I could smell his cologne. Lord, what that man did to me.

"We better get downstairs, or else no one will get to see how beautiful you are tonight."

"Why is that?"

"Because I'll be taking that dress off of you."

I grinned, and he took my hand to lead me out the door. Once we were in the hall, I could hear voices . . . lots of voices. All of a sudden, my muscles seized up, and my hands were sticky with sweat. Alex stopped to face me before we entered the library.

"I'm their boss, all of them. You are with me, so they will respect you. And I promise I will not leave you alone at any time, okay?"

"Okay," I said, smiling.

My hand clutched his arm, and as we approached the library, conversations came to a halt. Everyone blatantly stared at us. The large room was over the top extravagant. Fabric draped from the dark wooden bookshelves, and low lights gave the space an intimate feeling. Servers hurried around the room with trays of cocktails and Hor D'oeuvres and almost every guest wore a silky evening gown or tailored suit.

"Welcome to the 20th Annual Reed Banquet. I'm so honored to continue this tradition that my father started for our employees so many years ago. I do hope everyone will have a lovely time tonight. You've all earned it."

Everyone clapped and continued talking amongst their inner circles. Alex and I made our way around the room, and he greeted all of his employees. They talked about work, the island, and some took an interest in me. Especially men, which Alex always noticed. Being the alpha he was, his glare always resulted in them tucking their tails and shuffling away. I cut my eyes at him a couple of times, and he grinned knowingly.

One particular man, Jack, just couldn't take a hint. He tried to strike up a conversation with me several times, and Alex would always intervene. He stepped closer and closer to my side, and all of a sudden, he raised his hand and "accidentally" brushed across my breasts. Alex's jaw clenched as he turned to face Jack. The waves of rage that rolled off Alex terrified me and I was more than grateful that his anger wasn't directed at me.

"Sophia, can you grab us a couple glasses of wine while I have a chat with Jack?"

"Sure." I hurried into the next room to put as much space between us as possible. One thing I had learned about myself is that I did not like confrontation.

Several women gave me resentful and jealous glares when

I walked by, but I would have been shocked if they didn't. The man was quite a catch.

When I returned, Jack's head stayed down, and he did not make eye contact with me again. Alex smiled and talked to the group surrounding him like nothing had happened. He held the glass with one hand, and the other had a firm hold on my waist. Point made.

A well-dressed gentleman, whom I assumed was the Maître d', announced dinner, so we made our way to the main hall. There must have been fifty tables covered in white linen and fine china. The decor was elegant and classy. We sat at one of the front tables with some of the senior staff members from Alex's company.

They mostly asked Alex business questions during dinner, but it didn't stop him from being attentive to me. Leaning in to see if I needed anything, putting his arm around me, or making sure my glass stayed filled. When dessert came, I took the first bite of creamy cheesecake and let out an undignified moan. It tasted delicious.

Alex's hand squeezed my bare thigh, and I looked up to meet his very intense and longing gaze. I glanced around, realizing that everyone was staring. I already knew my face flushed red, and all I wanted to do was to crawl under the table. One of the men cleared his throat and continued speaking with Alex. But he never moved his hand. He made small light circles on my thigh, and they migrated higher and higher up the slit of my dress.

He stopped at the hem of the slit, trying to show some control. Control was the last thing I wanted from him that night, so I placed my hand on his and pushed it higher. His breath caught in his throat, then someone made the very loud announcement that the music and dancing had started in the next room. Lovely timing.

Everyone stood with excitement, and Alex turned his

head and stared at me with irritation. "Want to ditch them?" he asked.

"You can't ditch your own party," I said, laughing.

"I would for you."

"Oh, I believe you. But, I'm not going to let you do that."

He grumbled as he stood from his chair and led me to the dance hall. The party was in full swing, and every staff member kept busy dancing or drinking. They probably didn't get to cut loose like that very often and their enjoyment was obvious.

Upon entering the hall, I bumped into someone and turned to apologize. "I'm so sorry, I wasn't watching . . . Ian?"

"Sophia, you are beautiful as always. I'm so glad you're joining us tonight," he said politely. This was nothing like the angry Ian that stood on the cliff that night. He looked relaxed and handsome in a dark gray suit and black shirt. The impatient stares of the women nearby were evidence of Ian's reputation with the ladies; they were waiting their turn. For some reason, this didn't surprise me.

"Thank you, Ian, so good to see you as well," I responded. Alex barely acknowledged his presence and pulled me in the opposite direction.

"Maybe you can save me a dance later, Sophia."

Alex turned to glare at him. "Not gonna happen, Ian."

"We'll see," Ian smirked as he turned around.

I really wanted to inquire more about Ian, but that wasn't the time. Alex needed to focus on the banquet and his employees. The last thing I wanted to do was put him in a bad mood or cause a scene. He pulled me out on the dance floor when a rhythmic song came on, and I immediately started moving with him. I couldn't remember ever learning how to dance, but my body did. I closed my eyes and moved with Alex, clinging to every hard curve of his body.

"You're an amazing dancer, did you know that? The way

you move . . . it's very seductive." He leaned in with his mouth close to my ear. "Every man in here is watching you swing your hips and wishing they were me. I'm not sure if you've learned this, but I don't do well with others showing interest in what is mine. I'm quite territorial."

Alex grabbed my hand and pulled me from the floor. Guests attempted to speak to him on the way out, but there was no use. He had tunnel vision, and nothing could stop him. We got down the hall, away from the curious stares, and he turned me slamming my back against the wall. His mouth devoured mine before I figured out what was going on. He bit gently on my bottom lip and made his way down to my neck. His hand ran up my thigh, and when he reached under my dress, I could have collapsed right there. My vision grew hazy, and every nerve in my body was on high alert just by his touch.

Sensing someone nearby snapped me out of my trance as I peered down the hall. Ian wasn't even trying to hide that he was watching us. His body was stiff with tension and rage filled his eyes. The possibility that Ian had an interest in me before I started seeing Alex made me feel guilty. This wasn't something I wanted to rub in his face. I couldn't imagine what we looked like with me against the wall and Alex's hand under my dress. I quickly tapped him on the shoulder to get his attention, but when I turned back, Ian had disappeared.

"Are you okay? You know if this is too much for you, we can stop."

"No, it isn't that. It's just, well—Let's just go back to my room," I finally answered. Alex lightly kissed me and straightened my dress. We hurried down the hall to my room and barely made it through the door before he was all over me. Kissing. Pulling. Grabbing. Biting. I wanted every bit of it. I had wanted him for so long, this seemed like another dream. Alex turned me in his arms and unzipped the back of my dress. It fell to my feet, and his hands were on me instantly.

"Do you have any idea how often I have thought of this?" he asked. "The silkiness of your skin on mine, the taste of you on my lips. I'm going to take my time with you."

My breathing had gotten embarrassing, but I didn't care.

"You are so sexy, Sophia." This was wrong. I couldn't do this with him calling me Sophia. It felt like a betrayal.

"Please don't call me that."

"Why not? Did I do something to make you uncomfortable?"

"No, it's just awkward being this intimate with you and not remembering my name. I would prefer you didn't use one at all."

"Okay, gorgeous," he said as he nipped at my shoulder. Every nerve in my body electrified, and he ran over each one with his fingers. I kept waiting on something in my heart to tell me to not go through with it, or to wait a little longer. But, there was nothing. Nothing except want and need that I had been suppressing since I met him. He pushed me on the bed and climbed up my body, kissing all along the way. He took his time licking, biting, and tasting while staring at me with those green hungry eyes.

When he reached my lips, breathing hard, I squirmed for relief. Cradling the side of my face, he stared at me for several seconds. "I hope you know how much you've changed my life showing up here."

Tears filled my eyes, and I couldn't respond. Finally, he pushed into me. Alex paused to let my body adjust, then he took charge doing everything he said he would. That was precisely what I needed him to do. His hands gripped mine above my head and never relented, losing control in the best way possible. I completely surrendered.

I wasn't sure how long we stayed tangled up in bed

together. The amount of passion that had built up between us over the past month blew my mind. After a while, I relaxed on Alex's chest while he held me, the banquet forgotten, and all of his attention on me. Crashing waves echoed throughout the bedroom from the open window. I watched the ceiling fan slowly turn while thinking about my journey so far. I didn't know why, but something told me to relish the happiness I felt at that moment.

As if it would be short-lived.

8

MAY 25, 2020

Everything blurred. Why was everything blurry? Oh yeah! There was my new friend I'd just met. He was so sweet, buying me another round. He had the best sense of humor, and we talked for hours. We had so much in common. How much did I drink?

I don't feel so well.

What time should I be at my gate again? I'm supposed to be meeting someone, but I couldn't remember who.

"Have you had enough to drink?"

"Oh yes, I believe so," I slurred as I attempted to stand, but my balance was off and my new best friend held me up. He really was the greatest.

"All right, I got you. How about we go take a ride. Doesn't that sound like fun? We can talk some more along the way."

"That is soo seweet of you. Can yu driv mee hoome?"

"Of course, you know I'll take care of you," he reassured me. "Okay, I'm going to put my arm around you and help you to my car, alright? Then we'll take a short ride because I have a wonderful surprise for you."

"A suurplize? Oh that is windirful."

"Sir, can I help you with something? She doesn't look well," a strange voice called out.

"Well, officer, she's had a bad day and way too much to drink. I'm just trying to get her out of here and off your hands," he told my new police friend.

"Ma'am, is that true? Is everything all right?"

"Yes, surr. I haves a suurplize waitin."

"Get her home and make sure she stays there, okay?" He seemed annoyed. Maybe he could use a drink.

Should we invite him along?

"Yes, sir, that is my plan. Thank you for your concern."

We hobbled through the airport toward the waiting car. How lucky was I to meet this super nice guy that wanted to take care of me while I drank my cares away? As we were exiting the airport, I vaguely heard an overhead announcement. "Mrs. Brinkley, please come to gate eleven. Your party is waiting. Mrs. Brinkley to gate eleven."

Wait a minute. Something felt wrong about that. Why were they paging me? The situation felt off, but I didn't know why. I needed to go back and find out where I was supposed to be. I had to find someone to help me figure this out. Sophia. Where was she? I'm so confused. As soon as I tried to stumble out of my friend's grasp, he caught me and guided me into the back of a waiting car—where I passed out.

* * *

Present Day

MY BED WAS WARMER than usual. The sun had just started to rise, and sunlight peeked through the sheer curtains. I stretched, but something kept me from budging. It took me several minutes to remember what happened the night before and understand why I couldn't move. Alex draped across me. Of course, I was hot; he wasn't a small man. I tried to ease out from under him, but he pulled me back and smothered me with his body.

"You wouldn't be trying to sneak away from me, would you?" he asked.

"Well, not exactly. I have to use the restroom."

"Alright, but you'll be right back, right? I would hate to have to come after you," he said with irritation in his voice.

"Of course, I will. As long as you keep your grumpy morning-beast under control."

"Grumpy morning-beast?" He tried not to laugh.

Without answering, I slid out from under him and made my way to the bathroom. I stayed in there a little longer than necessary just to make him wait. I brushed my teeth and washed my face, taking extra time to moisturize and comb through the tangles in my hair. When I did return, he already had a tray of coffee and bagels waiting on the bed. He sheepishly smiled.

"That was fast. Are you trying to be extra sweet for being so demanding this morning?" I asked.

"Something like that," he admitted. He pulled me down on top of his chest. Running his hand down my body, he kissed me, then leaned back, studying my face with a serious expression. "How are you this morning?"

"I'm perfect. Why do you ask?"

"It's just after last night, I want to make sure there are no regrets. You have a lot going through your head right now, and I don't want to do anything to make things more difficult for you."

How could this amazingly sweet and attractive man be so self- conscious?

"Alex, I wouldn't have done anything that I wasn't one hundred percent sure about. I still feel that way this morning, I promise."

He smiled and kissed me once more before popping me on the rear and declaring, "Up woman, let's get you some coffee."

That was my kind of man.

After breakfast, we took a drive to the market for fresh seafood. Alex's staff usually handled all of the pick-ups, but we thought it would be a nice morning trip. Taking his jeep, he kept one hand on my thigh the entire time. I realized the contact brought him a sense of comfort. Not only was Alex very affectionate, but he was also super-observant. On the drive over, he must've noticed I was in my own world when he asked, "What is going on in that pretty head of yours?"

"I just wish I could remember my past so we could get to know each other better. I don't have anything that I can share with you."

"I'm sure it will come eventually. Dr. Carlos says it takes a while for the swelling to subside, and the memories would soon follow. He said the wound had healed beautifully when he removed your stitches."

I did remember him saying that, but I was impatient. "Can I ask you some questions?"

"Of course, I'm an open book for you." He winked at me and continued driving.

"You've mentioned your father several times, but never your mother. Is she still alive?" Alex shifted in his seat and cleared his throat uncomfortably.

"Wow, you're a straight shooter," he replied.

"I'm sorry if that is too personal. I'm just curious and . . . "

"Listen, gorgeous, you know how I feel about you. Just

because something is hard to talk about does not mean I don't want to share it with you."

I smiled at him appreciatively.

"My mom wasn't happy here. She didn't approve of my dad's business and wanted him to give it up. He explained to her that businessmen were ruthless, and if he wanted to succeed, he'd have to be the same. She said she would be leaving and taking me with her. She didn't want me to become like him, but it was too late."

"What do you mean too late?"

"I was already sixteen and old enough to see how the business worked. My father had been prepping me to take over one day, and my heart was set on it. No matter how horrible of a person he was, I still looked up to him. I'm not sure what that says about me." He muttered the last part so quietly I almost didn't hear him.

"So, she left?"

"She left.

"Alex, I'm sorry. But I'm glad you told me." I couldn't imagine how difficult it would be to have your mother walk away from you. I wondered about his father and why Alex looked up to him, but that is a conversation for another day. "Are you an only child?"

"I have a half-sibling, but I don't like to talk about it. It happened after my mother left, and I never really accepted it."

"Is it because you were hurt by your father? For being with someone other than your mother?"

"Maybe. Who knows?"

He pulled over and parked on the rough terrain. We stepped out of the jeep and started walking toward the market without another word. I brought up a lot of harsh memories for him and decided it was better if I let things go. I pulled on his hand, and he turned abruptly, confusion painted across his handsome face. Wrapping my arms around his neck, I kissed him hard and long. His shoulders relaxed under my arms, and I felt the tension leave his body.

He slowly leaned back and studied my face. "What was that for?"

"For being honest with me. I can't imagine how difficult that was for you to talk about."

His eyes were intense as he took his time, contemplating my answer. He kissed me on the forehead and continued walking toward the market. As we made our way toward the seafood dock, I spotted a hut with brightly colored woven wraps.

"Alex, can I meet up with you in a few minutes? I would love to take a look at those."

"Sure. Let me know if you find something you'd like."

Watching him saunter off toward the dock, I still couldn't believe he was the one who rescued me. I walked over to the wraps and immediately picked out a stunning green one, long enough to wear on the boat. The color reminded me of Alex's eyes.

"Well, it's about time you come back to see me," a familiar voice said. I turned to find Anna, smiling with her arms in greeting. She pulled me into a hug and held me for several seconds before leaning back and cocooning my face with her hands. "Now, where is my Alex?"

"He's picking up fish for dinner tonight, but he'll be right back. I actually came over here to try on your wraps. They are incredibly beautiful, Anna." I strolled in front of her table to inspect the others, but none of them compared to the green one.

"You like the green, yes?" she asked.

"I do. I think I'm drawn to it because it reminds me of Alex's eyes." I glanced back at her, and she stared with a weepy smile.

"Do you know how long I have hoped he would find someone who sees him like me? True love is challenging to find, my sweet Sophia."

True love? I wasn't sure I would go that far. I mean, I had very fond feelings for Alex, but I wasn't sure I knew what love was. Could I truly love someone I'd only known for a month?

"I can see the turmoil in your eyes. Take your time, my sweet girl. There's no need to rush emotions you don't understand. I'm just pleased he has something so wonderful in his life after all he has gone through."

"What do you mean?" I asked.

"Just family history, nothing for you to stress over."

"Anna, if you want me to be a part of this family, I want to know as much as possible about Alex."

Anna contemplated my words, and her shoulders relaxed in defeat.

"The tragedy with his mother was almost too much for him to bear. Then, of course, those horrible accusations against his father, and that bastard child almost ruined everything. He should've never had to deal with any of it at his age." She stared out in another world, and I imagined she was lost in a past she couldn't change for him. She seemed so much older to me right then. So much hurt and anger had built up for what Alex had endured.

"His mother? Alex told me that she left. I can't imagine the pain he went through."

"Yes, it was horrible. Officials searched and searched, but never found her boat. He went through a terrible grieving process. The child never got to say goodbye."

What? Grieving process? Alex never told me that part, but why? It would come across like I was digging for information if I started questioning her right then. And, what accusations against his father? My curiosity got the better of me, and I needed to know more.

"So Anna, I understand they never found his mother. I never really understood the accusations about his father. They seem a little wild to me," I lied.

"You're not alone there, sweet girl. Everyone knew that Richard Reed would never have touched that dirty Maria. She was nothing more than a slutty housemaid. For her to accuse a distinguished gentleman like Richard of a heinous crime like rape was absurd."

My mouth went dry, and my hands began to shake. I closed my fists to keep Anna from noticing. Alex's father was accused of rape? Now I knew why he didn't want to talk about him. Could it have been true? And what bastard child?"

"Ah! There's my handsome boy!" she exclaimed.

I turned to see Alex walking toward us, and he smiled at the sight of us together.

"Did you find everything you needed?" I asked.

"I did. Now I know why I send a staff member. I think I may have bought ten of everything."

"I'm sure the fishermen were grateful for it. This season has been hard on them," Anna replied.

"You know to contact me if anyone needs any help, Anna. We've talked about this."

"Yes. Yes. I know." She kissed his cheek before turning back to me. "Your lovely Sophia has taken an interest in this beautiful green wrap. I can't imagine why the color speaks to her so." She smirked, but Alex didn't notice.

"Sure. I mean, the color will be beautiful on her," he replied. "Make sure she gets it and anything else she would like to have." He snuck some cash to Anna, enough to pay for twenty wraps. He took care of her and the other locals on the island.

Anna wrapped everything to send with me. She packaged

the green wrap along with several handmade pieces of jewelry. After I promised to visit soon, we made our way toward the jeep.

"She's always so kind to me. There's a connection between us, and it feels like I've known her for years."

"Yes, Anna is the type of person that people can't imagine their life without. But, so are you." He reached over to hold my hand.

There was a comfortable silence on the drive home, both lost in our own thoughts. I didn't bring up anything about his father. I decided he would let me know when he was ready. I couldn't expect him to be patient with me if I couldn't show him the same respect.

"Did you go to Anna and Miguel when things got bad at home?" Hopefully, talking about them would be more comfortable than his parents.

"I did. Often," Alex replied. "They made sure I always knew I was loved. It didn't matter what I did wrong, I still felt like the center of their world. Everyone needs someone in their life like that. Everyone."

Today had been hard on Alex. Discussing his parents, and some of the experiences he had gone through made him tense and agitated. I changed the subject to lighten the mood.

"Do you know what else everyone needs in their life?" I asked as sweetly as possible.

"What's that?"

"Fish tacos from Mama Brenda's rust truck."

A surprised grin appeared on his face, and I instantly saw the stress dissipate. "Would you like some tacos?"

"Among other things."

"What things? You might as well tell me, you know I can't say no to you."

"Let's take our tacos to the beach, and we can go parking

afterward." Looking over with one brow raised, he turned the jeep in the opposite direction.

"Your wish is my command."

Anna might have been right, maybe my feelings were greater than I realized. I just wasn't sure how to know.

Darkness surrounded me. Between the sway of the boat and the throbbing pain in my head, I wasn't certain I could stand without falling. I pushed to my feet, baring my weight on the old wooden table. Slowly raising my hand to my head, I pulled back swiftly when blood, wet and sticky, coated my fingers. My stomach turned, and I fell to my knees, vomiting the last of whatever I had eaten. Heavy footsteps got louder, then stopped outside the door. I crawled across the rough wooden planks into the dark corner and tucked my knees into my chest, hoping I'd be less visible.

The door swung open, the creak of dry hinges the only sound, and a shadowy figure slowly walked in. His horrid presence penetrated the air as his head turned, searching the room. He walked from one side to the other. "Well, there you are. You're a pretty little thing, even if you are covered in vomit and piss," said a deep gravelly voice.

* * *

I BOLTED UPRIGHT in the bed, breathing hard and covered in sweat. The bedside lamp came on, and Alex was at my side in a flash. "What's wrong?"

"It was just a nightmare." I took several breaths, trying to calm my pounding heart.

"Do you want to talk about it?"

"No, but I'm going to take a shower and calm down before I can sleep."

"Okay, let me know if you change your mind. It might help." Alex kissed me on the head and laid back down, reluctantly.

I stood under the spray of the shower for a long while. I could smell vomit from the nightmare, and I scrubbed myself back and forth to erase the memory of it. Running my finger down the scar on the right side of my head, I closed my eyes at the flashbacks of being held hostage. Were those horrible visions of what I went through? If so, maybe I didn't want to remember.

I sank to the floor of the shower and sat under the spray with my knees bent. The nightmares were dark and dirty. No matter how long I sat there, I'd never feel clean enough. I was ashamed, even though it was just a dream. Something told me to stop living in denial. I knew it was real and I had actually been there with that horrible man. A heavy weight sat on my heart, and I knew that no matter what happened from there on out, I would carry guilt for ending up in that situation. It was there, heavy on my mind.

I still didn't know what took place or why it happened, but the fear I felt alone was enough to unnerve me. I sat in the shower until the water ran cold, and I forced myself to finally move. Chills covered my body from the frigid water. I grabbed my robe on the back of the door; its warmth traveled into my nerves and calmed me.

When I walked back into the room, Alex was spread out

across the bed asleep on his stomach. He slept with his arms above his head and I could see the muscles across his back and shoulders; I almost climbed back in bed. But, I figured I only had a couple of hours until sunrise, so I decided to get some fresh air and let him sleep.

I quietly made my way to the kitchen, praying someone was there to help me locate a cup of coffee. I smelled the delectable liquid before I saw it. As I turned the corner, Mary sat at the small wooden table with a mug of the mouthwatering brew in hand. She was all alone and seemed more peaceful and relaxed than I had ever seen her. I took a moment to observe her while she was unaware of my presence.

She had both elbows on the table, and her hands wrapped around her mug. Her eyes closed as she took small sips in the peaceful quiet of the kitchen. I almost felt guilty for interrupting her. Almost. I really needed some coffee.

She jumped up to stand when she noticed me. "Oh, ma'am. I apologize. What can I get for you?" she asked.

"Please don't apologize, Mary. After all, I'm the one who's disturbing you. I thought I might grab a cup of coffee and watch the sunrise this morning." An idea popped into my head, and I blurted it out before I had time to change my mind. "Would you like to join me?"

Mary stared at me like I wasn't all there. She slowly turned her head from one side to the other to make sure I wasn't speaking to someone else. "Me?"

"Of course. If you're busy, I understand. I just haven't had a chance to chat with you yet. This seems like a wonderful opportunity." *Stop being awkward.*

"Wow, of course. I mean, I would like that," Mary said, smiling. "My shift doesn't actually start for another couple of hours." She picked up her coffee mug and refilled it. Then she pulled down another cup for me and sat the cream on the

CHAPTER 9 | 103

counter. We grabbed our mugs and made our way out the back door of the kitchen.

Stopping at the edge of the lawn that met the gardens, she pointed out a small stone bench that overlooked the rock cliff for an unobstructed ocean view. It was ideal. We sat in comfortable silence for a few minutes, just taking in the breathtaking scenery.

"Can I ask you something, Sophia?"

I nodded for her to continue.

"Why did you ask me here?"

Her question stunned me. Do people not ask each other for coffee or for a small chat? Or did people not ask her? She thought I had an ulterior motive for asking her there, and the realization made me sad.

"Well, I hoped we could get to know each other. I know I'm quite a bit older than you, but I haven't had many people to talk to. It's a very lonely and isolating existence to not know who I am or anyone else for that matter."

Mary studied me while I spoke. When I finished, she turned her gaze back to the ocean, silent and focused. She was probably coming to her own conclusion about me before she opened herself up. How long had she been so guarded?

She turned back, engaged. "So, Sophia. What would you like to know?"

"Everything. Tell me all about yourself, Mary."

"Okay. Well, I have lived here as long as I can remember. As soon as I turned fifteen, Mr. Reed gave me a job so I could make my own living. He was always very kind to me, and I've missed him since he passed away."

She reflected on her past while staring out at nothing. I could tell by the blank gaze in her eyes that she was reminiscing. She quickly turned to correct herself.

"Don't get me wrong, the current Mr. Reed is nice as well.

But he can be very intimidating, and that makes me insecure, I guess."

"I completely get that. I was so afraid to speak to Alex the first time I met him. He can be very daunting. What about your parents?"

"I don't have any memories of them. They said I was found after a terrible boating accident and believe they were killed when the boat caught fire."

"I'm so sorry, Mary." That poor girl had lived here most of her life. That is all she knew, and it made my heart sad to think it was all she may ever know. I could tell she wasn't happy; she was just making it from day-to-day.

"What types of things do you do for fun?"

"I love this. Sitting out here in the morning watching the sunrise. Sometimes when I get done with everything in the kitchen, I borrow books from the Reed library, and I get lost in them for hours."

She was definitely my kind of girl.

"Reading is one of my favorite things to do, also. Reading and walking around the gardens give me a sense of peace. I absolutely love the flowers," I admitted.

"They are beautiful, but I'm not really familiar with them. I have tried to ask Ian to teach me, but he says he's too busy."

"I could have a chat with him about taking us on a tour one day."

"No, please don't. Honestly, Ian intimidates me also. I don't want him to know it, but I've had a huge crush on him ever since he came to work here." She blushed at the confession. "I'm not sure why he has to act like he is better than everyone. You would think him being an orphan like me, he would be more humble."

"Orphan? Ian is an orphan? I thought his father was the previous gardener?"

"Oh, Ms. Sophia, I'm so sorry. I shouldn't ever talk about

someone else's business like that. Especially since I come from nothing. I'm a horrible person for even mentioning it."

"Calm down, Mary. I promise anything you say is safe with me. We're friends, right?"

She smiled. "Yes ma'am. We're friends."

"So, I take it that he isn't the gardener's son?"

"No ma'am, he isn't. But the gardener did raise him. They were very hush-hush about Ian's real parents, and no one was allowed to talk about them. I don't think the younger Mr. Reed wanted Ian to act as our current gardener, but his father had already hired him before he passed. It would appear like Mr. Reed had gone against his father's wishes if he had fired him."

My mouth went dry, and my grip on the mug became tight. I thought about my previous conversation with Anna at the market.

"The tragedy with his mother was almost too much for him to bear. Then, of course, those horrible accusations against his father and the bastard child that almost ruined everything.

Then with Alex. *"I have a half-sibling, but I don't like to talk about it. It happened after*

my mother left, and I never really accepted it."

My God. Ian was Alex's half-brother. I couldn't believe I didn't pick up on it before. The competitive nature between them should've given it away. They didn't resemble each other, but they apparently had different mothers.

"Sophia, are you alright?" Mary asked.

I snapped out of my shock from the realization and plastered a smile on my face. I wasn't going to give anything away. It wasn't my secret to tell.

"Yes, I'm okay." I dropped the subject of Ian instantly, so I didn't say too much. I thought about this sweet innocent girl and how she trusted me enough to open up to me. I doubt many people sat and talked with her like this. "Listen, you've been so kind and honest with me. I want to tell you something that I haven't told anyone."

Her eyes widened, and she nodded for me to continue.

"I have nightmares that I believe are memories trying to come back. Horrible nightmares. And I don't believe my name is Sophia."

"Your memories are trying to come back? That's amazing," she exclaimed. "Do you have any idea what your name is?" she asked.

"I don't. I just know doubt hovers in the back of my mind about my identity when people call me Sophia."

"That has to be awful. I won't call you Sophia anymore. And, I promise not to tell anyone about your name or your memories. Not until you know for sure."

"Thank you, Mary. I would love for us to do this again soon. Maybe we can swap out books and discuss them over coffee," I offered.

"I would love that." Mary turned back to focus on the sea, and we sat in silence while we watched the sunrise. It was a splendid thing to behold as it rose above the water and signified a brand new day. Anything could happen. And I hoped that Mary believed the exact same thing.

She stood to leave, but turned back to face me. "I hope you know how much this meant to me this morning. I've never had a friend before, but something tells me that has changed." She smiled once again before turning back toward the house to begin her chores.

I liked this girl. I liked her a lot.

Heading back to our bedroom, I took a detour through the kitchen. Like always, the kitchen staff stopped and stared at me like I had three legs and a donkey tail. But then again, I still wore the fluffy robe I'd put on in the bathroom that morning.

"Good morning. I was curious if a tray had gone up for Mr. Reed yet."

Margaret spoke up. "No ma'am, we've been waiting to hear from him."

"Do you think it would be alright if I take it to him?" The kitchen staff looked at each other like I was an undignified stable-girl to ask such a thing. "It's just that I'm on my way back to the room, and I thought I could surprise him this morning."

"Of course, dear. I think that is a sweet gesture, and we will be more than happy to assist you," Isabel said as she came around the corner. "Won't we, ladies?"

"Oh, yes, ma'am. Very thoughtful indeed." Someone mumbled from the back. But, I could tell they thought I had lost my mind. Mary grinned over in the corner, and I gave her a wink.

"What exactly do you want for breakfast ma'am? We usually wait for Mr. Reed to give us his orders. If you want to wait, we can prepare it when he calls."

They didn't know me at all if they thought I would wait on his orders.

"That's okay, Margaret. I'm sure he will be fine with whatever I decide." You would think I had announced a hurricane was headed for the house. I smiled at their apprehension. It appeared that no one wanted to be a part of my plan, and it made me want to giggle. Were they really that afraid of him? That man was all bark and no bite.

"Do you have any more apple tarts, Margaret? They were delicious. And I'll take some coffee, fruit, and a slice of the quiche that is cooling on the stove."

"Yes, ma'am," Margaret said as she got to work. She handed me the tray like her job depended on it.

"Don't worry Margaret, I'll tell him it was all my idea."

"Thank you, ma'am."

I carried the tray to the bedroom, and before I knocked, I opened my robe at the top and pulled it down to show some cleavage. After a wild toss of my hair, I heard someone clear their throat. I swung my head to the side and saw Ian, pausing mid-step, his eyes taking in the scene before him.

He walked toward me, trying not to smile. "You know, my room is right down the hall. You can deliver breakfast to me anytime." He brushed a loose hair out of my face and walked away, leaving me red-faced and mortified.

Wonderful.

I knocked a couple of times. Seconds passed without an answer, so I banged harder.

"I didn't ask for anyone to bring anything, so this better be important," a groggy voice yelled. Angry stomping came toward the door, then Alex jerked it open.

"Oh, I'm sorry. Am I at the wrong door?" I asked seductively as I batted my eyes. Alex stood in nothing but a pair of running shorts and his hair stuck up in all directions. He leaned against the doorframe, enjoying the show.

"Now this is what I call service." He opened the door to let me in, and I tried my best to sashay into the bedroom. As he closed the door, I placed the tray on the table, and part of my robe fell from one shoulder. His stare followed my every move.

"Is there anything else I can help you with, sir?" I asked.

Alex slowly made his way around the bed. Never breaking eye contact, he untied the robe and let it fall. Early morning Alex is a very intense Alex.

"Oh, I'm sure we can think of something."

And he did. He thought of several things.

We spent the day on the sailboat again, and I was no better at it than I was the first time. He finally gave up and let me sunbathe while I re-read my favorite book. He said it was worth it so he could stare at me lying around in a bikini. Walking over every hour or so, Alex reapplied sunscreen to my shoulders, kissed me on the head, and went back to whatever he did on the boat. He anchored shortly after so we could lounge around together and have a glass of wine.

"I have a surprise for you today. Do you remember if you've ever gone snorkeling?"

"It doesn't sound familiar."

"It isn't difficult, and I think you'll enjoy it. I'll show you everything you need to know, okay?" He pulled out snorkels, masks, and flippers and gave me a quick run-through of the basics.

I was nervous, but I wasn't sure why.

"I'll stay right beside you, and if you need me, just give me a sign."

"Alright. Let's do this." I agreed.

We jumped into the water, and I briefly tested the snorkel out by sticking my face under the surface. The seal held tight, so I attempted to swim on top of the water like Alex had shown me.

He stayed by my side the entire time and pointed out various sea life. Coral, starfish, and lobster were plentiful. At one point, he tapped on my shoulder and pointed up ahead to a beautiful gliding stingray. I watched as it swam down and buried itself in the sand hiding from us. I kicked over to the boat and held on to the side of the ladder, taking deep breaths.

"Everything okay?" Alex asked as he joined me.

"Yes, this is breathtaking. I just got a little claustrophobic after a while, I guess."

"You did fantastic. We can go ahead and stop for the day, but I'll bring you out again soon."

"I'd like that." We unloaded our gear and settled back on the boat.

"I'm supposed to fly to Miami tonight, but leaving you is making me nervous."

"How long will you be gone?"

"I'll return tomorrow, but that's still twenty-four hours away." He made a point to stare at me with pitiful eyes, and an idea crossed my mind.

"Would you like for me to come with you?"

He didn't speak at first, as if he needed to weigh his options. I wasn't going to lie; I wanted him to want me there.

"The thought has crossed my mind, but I'm worried about the possible fall-out from it. Most of your trauma came from traveling, and I don't want to do anything to make you regress. It seems you're doing well with the structure here."

If Alex only knew how bad my nightmares were, he wouldn't think I was doing so well. There was a part of me that wanted to go with him. The thought of him being that far away from me would more than likely unnerve me. But, another part of me knew that this was his business trip, and he needed to focus. Plus, I had to function on my own. Right?

"I'll be fine, Alex. I promise. It's just twenty-four hours, and maybe it will make you realize that you can't live without me."

"Oh, I already know that." He stood and walked over toward me. He squatted down and tipped my chin so he could look into my eyes. "How are your nightmares?"

"They are about the same." I lied.

"So they're worse?" he questioned with a raised brow. I didn't answer, but I tried to look away. "You're lucky you're gorgeous because you can't lie for shit."

I was going to have to remember how perceptive this man could be.

"I'm okay. I'll let you know if it becomes too much to handle, okay?"

"If you think a change of scenery will help, you can sleep in my room. It's right down the hall from yours." Oddly, I hadn't even thought about his room before. He'd been in mine so much, I just thought of it as our bedroom.

"I don't think that has anything to do with it. Plus, I would rather stay where I'm comfortable if that's okay."

"Of course." He stood up and started to pull the anchor. When he did, several boats sped by with men in uniform. They were dressed for official business; similar to the other officers I had seen.

"More patrols," I said.

"Yes, unfortunately."

"Why, unfortunately?" It would seem like a good thing to have them close.

He turned to face me, and his expression changed to irritation. "I just hate that we need them, that's all. Crime has picked up recently. I won't even send my staff to the wharf alone. That's another reason I hate leaving you."

"I'll stay on the property, I promise."

He stared at me for a few seconds, judging my sincerity."

"Let's get back so I can pack for tonight. You know if you want anything at all, just tell a staff member. If you need me, Isabel knows to call immediately."

This overnight trip was stressing him out. I walked toward him, sitting in his lap. "I promise to call if I need anything." I leaned forward, kissing him softly. "You always take care of me, don't you?"

"I try. You don't make it easy."

10

Alex finally left for his trip. One would think he'd be gone for weeks the way he acted. I had to shove him out the door with Isabel grinning from ear to ear. After a quiet dinner in my room, I soaked in my favorite tub until my hands shriveled from the hot water. My plans included piling up in my beloved chair beside my favorite window and reading until bedtime. I opened the drawer to my nightstand and frowned. My book wasn't in the usual spot. It took me a few minutes to remember I'd taken it out on the sailboat earlier.

I planned on letting Mary borrow the novel the following day. The combination of a strong, smart, and courageous woman was exactly what she needed to absorb. I searched the room for my sandals and decided to make a quick run so I could finish the book that night. I paused, remembering the promise I made to Alex. But, the boat dock was located on his property and was well lit. It wouldn't take me long. Or, it shouldn't have.

The sun had set, and it was pitch black outside with just enough light coming from the docks to see where I was going. I sped up as fear urged me forward. It traveled under my skin, and chill bumps broke out across my arms. But, when I looked around, no one was there with me.

"You have to stop being so paranoid all the time," I told myself. I stood up straight and decided to make it quick before I gave myself a heart attack over nothing. I stepped over the wooden planks and cut to the right where it was anchored. A small hop and I landed on Alex's boat. My book was there, lying on the bench where I left it. I snatched it up and headed back toward the dock.

I traveled back the same way I came, but this time movement in the water caught my attention. I peered over the side of the dock, and a giant sea turtle swam close to the surface. I had never seen one so close, and the colors on the shell were mesmerizing. I'd have to remember to tell . . . *Oof!*

The breath was knocked out of my lungs, as the cold sea consumed me. My body froze in the dark water as fear revived my memory of nearly drowning in the ocean. My thoughts swirled in different directions. What was that? Was someone there? Convincing my mind to focus, I swam to the side of the dock.

You probably just slipped, leaning over the edge.

I reached both hands up to grab hold of the planks to pull myself back up. As soon as I did, a dark shadow stood over me, and a large hand came down on top of my head, pushing me under. My hands held their grip on the dock as I fought to stay above the water. I gasped to get air, but all I tasted was salt. They held a fistful of my hair, holding me down as I fought with everything I had to get free. The pain in my scalp was almost unbearable, where my previous head injury had been healing.

My fingers clawed into the dock, and pieces of wood splintered off under my nails. As soon as I could pull away enough for them to loosen their grip without falling in, I pushed to the surface to take a breath. When I did, a fist came flying across my face, and my vision went in and out. I would die at the hands of my attacker, or the ocean would finish what it started that night. My mind only saw those two options.

A voice yelled in the distance. Was I screaming? No, that wasn't me. But, I knew the voice. Suddenly, someone pulled on my arms, trying to lift me onto the dock.

"You have to help me, I can't do this by myself," the voice cried.

Mary. It was Mary.

"Somebody help us!!" she yelled. "Over here! Please hurry!"

Several footsteps ran across the dock, then strong arms pulled me from the ocean. I coughed up the water I had taken in, but my vision still blurred.

"Dear Lord! What has happened here?" Isabel yelled. "Is she breathing?"

"Yes, she's breathing," someone answered.

"Get her inside and call Dr. Carlos. Someone needs to survey the area to see if anyone is on the property that isn't supposed to be here," Isabel demanded.

Someone I did not recognize spoke up. "Who is going to call Mr. Reed?"

Everyone got very quiet. Someone picked me up and carried me across the yard.

"It's okay, Sophia. I have you now." It sounded like Ian.

His tenderness surprised me. He came across so tough and callous at times. But, that had more to do with Alex than myself. I tried to remember what exactly happened out there that night. I couldn't get a good view of his face, and it frustrated me to no end. My eyes were heavy, and I started giving into sleep as I leaned my head on Ian's shoulder.

"Rest, I've got you."

I woke briefly when he laid me on the bed. I was aware of several people in the room, but I wasn't sure who.

"Dr. Carlos is on his way. It won't take him long," Isabel announced. "We need to get her out of those wet clothes. Mary, you stay and help me. The rest of you wait outside."

People shuffled out the door, and Isabel spoke again. "Ian, you need to wait outside also. Now," she said with authority. I heard the door close, and I assumed everyone had gone.

Isabel helped me sit up so they could remove the wet clothes. "Dear, sweet Sophia, what happened to you tonight?" Isabel questioned as she undressed me. "Mary, what did you see?"

"Well, Um. I wanted to get some fresh air before bed, so I sat down to read on the bench right before she walked out. That's how I knew it was her. She was on the side of the dock with the broken light, so I could barely make anything out. But I heard shuffling, and I had a bad feeling. I saw a shadow of someone standing by the boats, so I took off toward her. They ran off when I started screaming, but I don't know where. I just needed to get to her," she cried.

"Alright, alright. That is enough tears, young lady. You saved Sophia's life tonight, and heroes do not cry."

I heard Mary quiet her sobs. I couldn't wait to hug her neck. She had no idea how grateful I was for her. She ran out there with no thought of her own safety and could have been killed.

Isabel grabbed Alex's large shirt that laid across the bed from earlier that day and put it over me. I was thankful for the loose fabric, and the comfort it would bring from smelling like him. A few minutes later, a knock sounded, and Dr. Carlos stepped inside. His clothes were disheveled, and his comb-over went in the opposite direction. Poor Dr. Carlos.

"Sweetheart, are you trying to give me a stroke?" he asked.

"Then I hear Mr. Reed isn't home . . . I'm going to need to give him a sedative when he gets back, so he doesn't kill someone!" He took out a handkerchief and wiped the sweat from his brow.

"I'm so sorry they called you. I think I'm going to be fine."

"I'll come out anytime to check on you, but you have to keep yourself out of trouble. Especially when that man of yours is out of town. Understand?"

"Yes." I threw my arm over my eyes, knowing Alex would go crazy.

He was right. Alex had been worried about leaving, and I couldn't stay in my room for one night to give him peace of mind. Dr. Carlos evaluated my previous head injury and said it wouldn't need any more stitches. I had a bruise starting to shadow my left cheekbone, but it didn't seem like anything was fractured.

Someone knocked on the door, and Isabel answered it. They handed her a cell phone, and she took a deep breath before answering, "Yes, sir? I'm not sure, sir. Of course. Yes, sir. Right away, sir. I'll make sure they are expecting you. I'm very—" She paused, staring down at the display, and then handed the phone to a gentleman I had never seen. "Please make sure you're at the airport in three hours to pick up Mr. Reed."

"Yes, ma'am." The man turned to leave as though Isabel had a whip in her hand.

"He doesn't have to come back early. Really I'm okay." Every head in the room spun toward me like they almost forgot I was there. "My head is starting to clear, I'm not quite as dazed as I was."

"And while that is good news, we don't want to push it," Dr. Carlos spoke up. "Why don't you get some rest, and you can call me tomorrow to update me. If anything seems worse or abnormal, then I'll come back in. Otherwise, you should heal up fine. You're fortunate to be alive." He ran his hand down the back of my head in a fatherly way, then made his way out of the room.

"Dr. Carlos?" I yelled across the room before he walked out.

"Yes, Sophia?"

"Thank you. Thank you for always being here for me. I mean, I know it's your job, and you get paid to take care of me. But, something tells me you would do it anyway."

He smiled, and this time it reached his eyes. "Get some rest, Sophia." Then, he was gone.

I woke in the middle of the night, and heaviness hung in the air. Frustration and tension throughout the room told me I wasn't alone. Alex sat in the armchair by the window with a drink on one knee. His other hand rubbed his chin back and forth while he watched me. The moonlight streamed in over his features just enough that I could see the weariness in his eyes. Slowly, I sat up and reached my hand out for him to come to bed. He watched me intently but did not move.

"Alex?" Several seconds of silence passed and I tried again, "Alex, are you okay?"

"I shouldn't have left you," he responded.

The glass turned up, and he finished what was left of his drink. After placing the glass on the table, he ran his hand through his hair. He still wore the suit he'd left in, the coat and tie lost along the way. The top buttons of his shirt were not fastened, and the sleeves were awkwardly rolled up. I'm not sure I had ever seen him so out of sorts.

"Something told me when I left here yesterday that things were going too good for me right now. Something whispered that I would lose you like I've lost everyone else in my life. I brushed it off as my insecurities rose to the surface. I can't lose you when I just found you. I won't."

I stood up from the bed and walked across the room

toward him. Snuggling into his lap, I laid my head against his chest as his arms wrapped around me. I knew why he didn't come to bed when I felt the uncomfortable pressure he exerted. Whether it was from anger or anguish, he didn't trust his control.

"Alex, you're hurting me."

His arms loosened, and he tried to relax his body.

"This isn't your fault. No one could have known something like that would happen."

His silence continued, as he stayed deep in his own self-loathing and guilt.

"But, you're here now, and that is all that matters."

He kissed the top of my head, and we sat together by the window, knowing it could have ended very differently.

"I want you to know that I have the best investigators on this. I'll find out who attacked you, and they will pay for it," he said with a deadly tone.

I wasn't sure how long we sat together, but I found myself drifting off to sleep again.

A knock at the door snapped us out of our private moment. I sat up to stretch my back, and realized how sore I would be from the struggle at the dock. "I'd like to get a shower. I still smell the seaweed, and it isn't doing anything for my stomach.".

"Okay. Go grab a shower, and I'll get the door." He kissed the top of my head, then I made my way to the bathroom.

I walked into the room, and the sight in the mirror caused me to gasp. Dried blood caked the side of my head, and a large bruise shaded one side of my face. The tiny crack in the glass once again pulled me from my despair. The broken piece still remained. *You can't ignore it.* As I turned away from my reflection, refusing to dwell on it any longer, I clenched my fists and a sharp pain shot through my fingers. My nails were painfully embedded with dirt and tiny splinters of wood. I searched the cabinet for tweezers and started to remove what I could.

The memory of digging into the dock repeated in my head and tears ran down my face. I could barely get the splinters out for shaking. A light knock sounded on the bathroom door.

"Sophia, is everything okay? You've been in there a while, babe."

I sniffed, trying to compose myself before I answered, "Um . . . Yes. I'm fine. I'll. Um. I'll be out soon, okay?"

The doorknob turned, and I looked up to see him staring, scrutinizing the situation before him. His eyes were full of anger at the sight of me in the light, but it was soon replaced with sympathy at my current situation.

"Can I help?"

"I really don't want you to see me like this."

"I wasn't here to protect you or take care of you last night. Let me do that now."

Alex squatted down in front of me and took my hands in his. He stared at my fingers and tried to hide the fury simmering to the surface.

"Did Dr. Carlos not see this last night?"

"I think he was concerned with the bleeding and possible head injury."

He nodded thoughtfully, and then took the tweezers to gently remove the large pieces he could reach. My hands shook uncontrollably.

"Am I hurting you?"

"No, you're much better at it than I am." He pulled the majority out, then washed my hands over the sink so he could see what remained. He opened the drawer and found a pair of nail clippers, cutting my nails down to the tips of my fingers one by one.

"Shorter nails will be easier to clean and will hopefully

heal quicker." He clipped as much as possible, then Alex took me back to the sink and poured an antiseptic over my hands. "Let's get you in the shower and keep a watch on your hands for redness. If there are any more splinters, you'll be able to feel them." He helped me undress, then guided me into the shower.

To my surprise, he shed his clothes and stepped in behind me. I stood under the spray, vulnerable and tired. Alex knew me well enough to pick up on my emotions, and he did everything for me. I wasn't sure who needed it more, him or me. He gently scrubbed my hair around the tender area, then washed my sore body, so I never had to move. Afterward, we stood under the water, and he held me while I just breathed.

As we stepped out of the shower, he grabbed the plush robe and wrapped it snug around my shoulders. While he focused on the tie at my waist, I stared at this wet naked man taking care of me. My gaze traveled down his body, and when I peeked back up, he fought a grin. "Don't even think about it." Even though I knew it was for the best, I still gave a pouty smirk.

"Who was at the door?" I asked.

"Isabel, with your morning coffee."

I smiled, and he shook his head back and forth while chuckling.

"Wow. I see how quickly you forget about me."

"Well, you've already turned me down. Coffee never will."

We settled back into the bedroom, and Alex questioned me about the events from the previous night. "You promised me you wouldn't leave the property."

"Well, technically, the dock is on the property." It wasn't my smartest answer, and I regretted it instantly. "I am sorry, Alex. It was only supposed to take two minutes, and I could even see the house from the dock. All I wanted to do was grab my book and come back to my room. I never meant to lie to you or put myself in danger."

"This book?" He handed me the book I went searching for.

"Where did you find that?"

"On the dock. I guess you dropped it before falling in. I went out there, scouring around when I arrived home last night."

I held the book to my chest, thankful he had recovered it. I discreetly opened it to make sure the scrap of paper was still tucked inside. Thankfully, it was there.

"Have you slept at all?" I asked, noticing the dark circles underneath his eyes.

He shook his head no."What happened out there? And don't change the subject."

I exhaled and dread came over me at having to recall the details.

"I need to give the investigators everything. There is a high probability one of the villagers you made friends with came back to finish what he started. I need to know every detail."

The villagers. The thought never occurred to me that they would still be a threat.

"I felt as though someone was watching me, but I tend to be paranoid anyway. On my way back, I saw a sea turtle, and as I leaned over to watch it, someone pushed me in."

He stared at me, unmoving, and I knew he wanted me to continue.

"As I reached up to pull myself out, someone held my head under water. I tried to escape, but they were too strong. I tried to wiggle free, but they hit me across the face."

Alex couldn't sit still any longer, so he started pacing the room. I had just finished telling him about Mary trying to pull me up when we were interrupted by someone at the door. He went to answer it, and upon opening, his body grew stiff, and his voice was laced with loathing.

"What do you want, Ian?"

"I just wanted to check on our patient, boss."

Uh oh.

"I think I can handle things from here, and I'm sure you have work to do."

I felt bad for Ian. After all, he did carry me back from the dock.

"Ian?" I asked timidly.

Alex turned around with an annoyed expression across his face.

"Sophia, I just wanted to check on you. You look so much better than you did last night. You had us so worried, sweetheart. I wanted to apologize that Isabel made me leave when you begged me to stay with you."

I didn't remember that part, but I let it go. I wasn't sure why Ian tried to rile Alex up, but I couldn't deal with it that day.

"Ah, yes, well. Thank you for your assistance, Ian. I appreciate all of you. I didn't want you to leave without hearing that. I stepped back to let him know the conversation was finished.

"I see you were able to get a shower and out of that shirt. I'm sure you're way more comfortable. We had the hardest time getting you out of your clothes last night," he said with a grin toward Alex.

"I'm sorry, *what?*" Alex demanded as he stepped forward.

I put my hand on Alex's chest, knowing Ian was just jealous. He was hurting, and he wanted Alex to suffer also.

"Well, I'm not sure I could have showered without Alex doing all of the work. I'm lucky to have such a sweet and caring man to take care of me. Have a nice day, Ian."

I shut the door and turned to Alex. His eyes blazed, and

his hands were clasped behind his head. I honestly think he was afraid he would hit something if he moved.

"I never begged him to stay, and he wasn't there when Isabel and Mary changed my clothes. You have my word."

He only gave me a slight nod. "He'll regret it if he keeps pushing me."

Something tells me he's right.

11

MAY 25, 2020

I roused when the car started to slow but gave nothing away. Lying as still as possible, I replayed the last few hours in my mind. Something about being at a pub in the airport and Sophia was on her way to meet me. A handsome stranger joined me, and we passed the time drinking and chatting. He was there on business. I think he told me he worked in sales, but that's all I could recall. He was interested in me, asking if I had a husband or boyfriend. I was sure he wanted to ask me out until I drank too much. Or did I?

I'd never been one to binge drink where the ability to walk and talk left me, so I knew with all of my heart that wasn't what happened. Did he slip something into my beer? Am I one of those naïve and trusting young women that would drink something a total stranger bought her? My humiliation and guilt over the situation told me I deserved whatever I got. Am I the woman who never imagined this would happen to her? The woman I used to mock for being irresponsible? Look how quickly it happened.

The car lurched to a complete stop, and doors opened quickly. I was pulled to the door by my legs and lifted into the strong arms of a stranger. Was this the same man at the pub? I couldn't tell.

"Wow, she's a nice one," a rough gravelly voice stated. "She still out?"

"She's out. I thought about keeping this one for myself, but the offer is too high."

That voice. The man I just spent hours with. The creak of wooden boards on a dock whined under his feet as the breaking of waves sounded through the night air. If they got me on a boat, I might never get away.

"Let's get her situated, so we can leave when he gets back." The man with the rough voice mumbled.

"Sounds good to me."

They carried me to a seating area and laid me on a soft bench. After a few seconds, I peeked my eyes open and saw the back of an older man preparing the boat to leave. I slowly sat up and surveyed my surroundings. The guy from the airport didn't appear to be around, so I stood as quietly as possible and tested my balance. I felt dizzy and lightheaded, but the adrenaline pulsing through my body helped me push through. Searching for an exit, I took a few steps forward.

Creak. Creak.

"Hey, you! Stop right there!"

I ran toward the railing as fast as I could with the old man on my heels. Jumping toward the dock, I stumbled but caught myself from falling completely. His boots stomped against the wood behind me and his breathing was labored. My lungs screamed, and my muscles ached, but I had to get to Sophia.

I pushed forward as hard as I could down the dock and turned a sharp corner into an empty parking lot, as panic rose up my throat. A hard, unforgiving body stopped me in my tracks, and his grip kept me from stumbling backward. "Now, where do you think you're going?" he asked.

"Please, please don't do this. Sophia is waiting for me at the airport. She will know something isn't right when I don't meet her," I pleaded.

"Sophia, huh. How about I go wait for your friend, and she can come with us?"

"No! Leave her alone. Please." I begged. "You don't have to do this. Please don't do this. I'll do . . . I will do . . . whatever . . . the sharp sting hit my arm, and I heard the amused voice of the old man.

"That should do the trick. If you're getting another one, best get on it. We're leaving soon."

* * *

Present Day

THE SUN'S blistering rays beamed down as we made our way to the market. At least I had shorts on; poor Mary had worn black pants. We were more than delighted when Alex arranged for us to walk together that morning. Giving her the day off with pay was his way of showing gratitude for saving my life.

"He smiled at me," Mary said. "He's never done that before."

"Well, maybe this will change things for you. Having the boss on your side has to be a good thing, right?"

"I sure hope so."

"Alex gave me cash and said to get anything we'd like," I assured her.

Mary's eyes lit up with excitement. The thought crossed my mind that this could very well be her first shopping trip. I had only seen her working or reading, and the books must've belonged to the Reed library. I wanted to make sure she did things like this more often. Things girls her age would do.

We were given a particular path to walk down by Alex, but there wasn't a need for it. Mary knew exactly where we were going, and she wouldn't let us get lost. After another half hour of walking, we arrived at the center of the crowded market. The place buzzed with energy. There were typically ten to fifteen huts set up outside the wharf. But on that day, there had to be at least thirty. Not just the usual bright clothing and jewelry, either. There were fresh fruits, baked desserts, and crafts made from coconut hulls. Anna and Miguel flagged us down, so Mary and I weaved through the crowd to their table first.

"There's my beautiful Sophia! Come! Come! I have much to show you today."

"Anna, do you know Mary?"

Anna regarded Mary with disdain, then focused back on me. "What is this business of you being attacked?" She turned my head from side to side, inspecting the faded bruises on my face.

"I'm fine, I promise. I wouldn't be if it weren't for Mary, though. She saved my life." Mary's head lowered uncomfortably. What was it with her and Anna?

"Yes, well. I'm just glad you're okay sweet girl. I don't know what my Alex would do without you." She directed us toward her new fabrics, and when I turned, Mary had already moved on to a different hut.

"Anna, I need to be going. The market is packed today, and we have some shopping to finish up." I showed her the items I'd chosen, and she wrapped them enthusiastically.

"Yes, Sophia. All of these tourists are trying to cheat me out of a dollar . . . Everyone wants to swindle you out of a living these days." Anna shook her head from side to side, exasperated.

After kissing Anna on the cheek, I turned to make my way toward the other tables. The variety of fresh fruits and vegetables were overwhelming. The market was full of energy, and I could sense the eagerness of the locals. This was their way of life; the way they fed their families. People were everywhere, perusing handmade clothing, bags, and jewelry. I stumbled backward when I ran into a couple of tourists walking toward me.

"I'm so sorry!"

"Oh, it's no problem. There are so many people out today, it's difficult maneuvering from hut to hut," the woman said.

Middle-aged and decked out in tropical shirts and straw hats, they smiled brightly at me as if they'd made a new friend. That is until the man did a double-take and studied me uncomfortably. His wife cleared her throat, but he kept gawking.

"Sweet Jesus, Herb, you're embarrassing me again," his wife scolded.

"I'm sorry, Betsy. It's just that she seems so familiar." He continued to stare.

This is awkward.

"Look around you, Herb. God made lots of women with brown hair." She rolled her eyes.

"Ma'am good luck with your shopping. I'm going to get my husband out of here, I think he's had too much sun for one day," she said apologetically. She grabbed him by the arm and pulled him toward the docks.

He looked back as he whispered, "Betsy, I think that's the woman on the news." When I spun around to question him further, his wife squinted, her eyes studying me.

"No, Herb, she just favors that reporter from California. Leave the poor woman alone." Betsy had her hands full with Herb, no doubt. News reporter? I must resemble some famous news anchor. But, if there's a chance . . . I turned to find out more, but they were lost in the crowd. I walked around for several minutes, but I was unable to locate them.

I found Mary in the crowd, and she shyly admitted she'd seen a dress she'd like to have. "I only ever wear pants, so it would be nice to have something else. And, I don't know when I'll get a chance like this again," she said quietly.

The vibrant sundress she pointed out a few huts down was a lovely shade of pink, and the length would hit around her knee. It was modest but cute and it would be perfect for her age. I bought her two of them in different colors and a necklace to match. With tears in her eyes, she offered a quiet thank-you and refused to let me buy anything else.

I found handmade soap, mangoes, and I snuck off to buy us a couple of sun hats to wear back home. The sun was brutal. When I walked back over to where Mary waited, she shifted uncomfortably.

"What's wrong?" I asked.

"Um. It's just those men are here. They are never around this part of the island, and they are making me nervous."

My gaze followed the direction Mary focused on, and I saw him, the villager that held me hostage. My stomach dropped, and I froze in my tracks.

"Are they supposed to be here?" I asked.

"It's a public market, so I can't see why not. But they do scare me."

The villagers walked toward the exit of the market, right beside us. The leader raised his chin and made eye contact with me, but I couldn't make myself look away. A surprised expression crossed his face, and he immediately lowered his gaze to the ground and continued walking.

"Wow, I've never seen them lower their eyes to anyone before," she said thoughtfully.

I thought the same thing.

"Alex questioned their involvement over the attack at the dock."

"Do you really think they could have had something to do with that? It would be strange for them to attack outside their territory," she said.

"I don't know, but they are gone now, so let's head back to the house." I handed her the hat, and she smiled as I put mine on.

"I can't believe you bought me this hat," she said in shock. "You spent too much."

"Just enjoy it, Mary. Alex expects us to buy some things, and we wouldn't want to disappoint him, would we?"

We gave each other a grin that said this was between us. We walked in comfortable silence for a while, but I couldn't stop thinking about the man at the market. He was so sure he knew me.

"Mary, did you see the American couple at the market?"

"I'm not sure. That place was packed with tourists today. Why do you ask?"

"No reason. Just curious." I decided to leave it alone.

THE NEXT DAY, I sat outside in the garden, waiting for Alex to return from a factory visit. The sun was hot, but not quite as vicious as it was the day before. I bent my head back, closed my eyes, and allowed the breeze to blow over my skin. Things had been so pleasant lately. Alex's mood had improved, and Mary opened up more and more to me. The only thing that got under my skin was the scornful vibe that radiated from Ian. It had to be jealousy over his older brother; there was no other reasoning behind it.

Several boats made their way to the fisherman's market, and intuition told me something had happened. I stood at the edge of the garden, using my hand to block the sun so I could get a better view. It was difficult to tell from the house, but they looked official. I watched as they docked, and several men made their way to the island. Interesting.

Sweaty from the sun, I decided to grab a shower before Alex got home. I took my usual route through the back door of the kitchen, where the staff was huddled up whispering.

"Hi, everyone," I greeted.

Most of them were not very social, but I kept trying. They all stared, and the conversation stopped mid-sentence.

"Hi, Ms. Sophia," I heard someone say.

"Does anyone know what is going on at the wharf?"

A chorus of, "No," "No ma'am," and "I don't know," sounded through the kitchen.

Strange women. I made my way down the long hall toward my room, then stepped into the restroom to wash up. Afterward, I found a pretty sundress to wear for Alex. The last time I wore something showing off my legs, he said it was hot. I hoped for the same reaction today. I left my hair down the way he liked it and added some color to my cheeks and lips.

On my way out, I heard muffled voices through my open window. I took a peek, and saw several officers interviewing Ian on the lawn. I couldn't hear what they said, but Ian pointed around the property while speaking with them. Alex must have just arrived home. He walked across the lawn to meet them.

"Can I help you?" That's all I heard, but Alex's voice was tense. A passing ship muted the rest of the conversation. Alex dismissed Ian and dealt with the uniformed men himself. I wasn't sure what they discussed, but Alex wasn't happy. I was positive he didn't appreciate them on his property. It took a little while for the officers to leave, but they finally started back toward the market and Alex made his way inside the house. I opened the door to wait for him, knowing he would come to me first. After a minute or two, his voice echoed in the hallway.

"What in the hell do you think you're doing?" Alex asked.

"I don't know what you're talking about."

"Watch your back, Ian. You're not going to like where this is going with us."

I closed my door quietly and waited. After a few minutes, Alex entered and smiled at the sight of me. "Wow. Beautiful as always." He rushed across the room and wrapped his arms around me.

"Thank you." I kissed him hello and pulled back to study his face. "Are you okay? I saw the officers outside."

He stared down at me, deep in thought while chewing the side of his lip. "Yes, I'm fine, gorgeous. They were just searching for someone, but I'm not sure who. I've never heard of them."

"Oh, okay. I thought maybe the police had heard something." I could tell by his expression he wasn't following.

"About my disappearance."

"Oh, no, I'm sorry. I haven't heard anything." He stared at me with sorrowful eyes. "For what it's worth, I couldn't be happier that you are stuck with me."

He leaned down toward me again, and his lips took mine as if they would never kiss me again. Desperation and hunger flowed through Alex, and I allowed him to take what he needed. His mouth and hands were more urgent than usual, but I didn't mind. He had my dress by the handful, and his teeth grazed across my bottom lip. His mouth became greedy, and he jerked my body into his, guiding me back toward the bed.

His hand quickly reached between us to unzip his pants. Lying down on top of me, he fought to raise my dress. He pushed into me with urgency and need. It was the most aggressive Alex had been with me so far. It didn't scare me, but I could tell something was off. It almost felt territorial; he needed to confirm I belonged to him. He finished quickly and pulled out, with little regard to what I needed. I didn't believe it was on purpose, because I could tell his mind was elsewhere. Alex wasn't there with me that day.

He collapsed on the bed beside me, staring at the ceiling. "Did I hurt you?" He asked so quietly, I almost didn't hear him.

"No, I'm fine. Are you okay, though? You aren't quite yourself."

He turned toward me and gently swiped a hair that had fallen in my face. He then pulled the bottom of my dress down to cover me. My tender and sweet Alex had returned.

"I'm much better now." He leaned down and kissed me softly.

"Promise me. Promise me if something is wrong, you'll talk to me."

"You don't have anything to worry about, babe." He stared at me for a minute, and concern crossed his face. "Are you sure you're alright? Do you swear I didn't hurt you?"

"I'm fine. It's just . . . " I paused, trying to find the words.

"What?"

"Well, you've been preoccupied with the investigation, and now with the officers on the island, you're a million miles away. I would like some time with you, you know?" I hoped deep down I didn't come across as a needy girlfriend.

Alex smiled and leaned in to kiss me. "I'll tell you what, I'll be here tonight at eight to pick you up for a date. Just the two of us."

He waited on my response, and a smile spread across my face.

"Really? Like a real date?"

"Like a real date."

* * *

SEVERAL HOURS LATER, I found that I was the typical woman buried knee-deep in clothes screaming she had nothing to wear. The realization humiliated me. My hair curled, my makeup sultry, and I stood stark-naked in the bathroom in a pair of stilettos. I'd narrowed it down to either a cocktail dress or a dressy sleeveless black romper.

I pulled the romper down from the hanger and tried it on. This was probably my safest bet. The top ruffled down the front, and the bottoms were short enough to be sexy, but still classy. The stilettos made my legs look hot. Win-win.

I wore the necklace Alex bought me, and had just finished clasping a bracelet when he knocked.

"Coming!" I hurried to open the door but stood surprised to find Ian standing before me.

"Hey, wow. Nice outfit. What's the occasion?"

"Date night." I smiled with anticipation.

"Right. Well, I'm just going to be blunt. What do you see in Alex? It's just that I keep waiting for you to wake up and see you are too good for him. You can do better."

"Like you? Is that what you mean?"

Ian ground his teeth, and a tense expression crossed his face. "Maybe."

I felt sorry for him, I really did. "Ian, I appreciate the advice, but. . ."

"What advice?" Alex said as he walked up the hallway. Neither of us spoke, so he repeated the question. "What advice?" He stared Ian down until he submitted, and his eyes lowered to the floor.

"Just that it's supposed to be cool tonight. Sophia might want to take a jacket." A sad and hurtful expression crossed his face, then he covered it just as fast. "Excuse me, you two have fun."

Just like that, he was gone. I struggled with how to respond to Ian. I would never want to hurt him, but he needed to learn some boundaries.

"What was that about? Because I think you know I didn't buy the jacket excuse."

"I'm not sure."

"Damn, babe. Those legs." Grabbing me by the waist, he pulled me toward him and showed me what he thought of my outfit. "Are you hungry?" I know he's talking about food, but his eyes narrowed as though he might eat me for dinner.

"I'm always hungry," I said.

Alex smirked and led me down the hall.

As we exited the front door, my eyes caught a glimpse of the long black limousine waiting for us. Alex opened the door to the back and waited for me to get in.

"This is for us? Are you serious?" I asked, laughing.

"You're killing my confidence, woman. I'm trying to impress you here." He watched me expectantly. I wiped the grin from my face and threw my hand over my chest dramatically.

"Oh, Alex, I can't believe it. Is this limo really for me? This has to be the most perfect date ever. What a charming, classy, rich man you are." I said, trying not to smile.

"Are you accusing me of throwing my money around to impress you?"

I strolled toward him, never breaking eye contact, and when I stood inches from his face, I lightly kissed the corner of his mouth. "You don't have to do anything to impress me. Just promise to always look at me like that every time I walk toward you." I kissed him once more and climbed in the back seat of the limo.

We pulled up to a restaurant and were escorted inside to a private table. Everything in the entire place, from the decor to the lighting, was turquoise blue. A gentleman came to the table immediately with wine and hurried back the way he came.

"He forgot to leave a menu."

"They don't have menus at Turquoise."

"How will I know what I want to order?"

"The chef decides the special for the night, and that's what everyone eats."

"What if I don't like it?" I asked, confused.

"Oh, you'll like it. The chef here is a genius, and everyone always loves it."

Alex was correct, as usual. The waiter brought a plate of lobster and scallop linguine in a white wine sauce, and my taste buds exploded. An undignified moan escaped me, and Alex tried to suppress his grin. "Genius?"

"Is he single?" I asked.

The question went unanswered, but I did receive a rather nasty smirk.

I finished my entree quickly, and a creamy chocolate soufflé soon followed.

"I better get you out of here before you find yourself a boyfriend in the kitchen." Alex smiled, amused at my eagerness over the delectable dessert. As we left the restaurant, a building across the road caught my attention. Flashing lights and loud music begged to be noticed.

"What is that?"

"Pedro's? That would be the hottest night club on the island." He continued walking, but I stood there, observing the long line of people dying to get inside.

"Would you like to go?" He watched me closely.

"Really? You would do that?"

"I've seen you dance. Of course, I will."

"Yes, of course, I want to go." We walked across the street, and I headed to the back of the line to wait. Alex put his hand around my waist and directed me to the front.

"Carlos, how are you, my friend?" Alex said.

"Alex! It's been too long. Pedro will be pleased you're here. Please, please come in." He opened the rope so we could walk through, and I cringed at the remarks from the people waiting in line.

"A friend of yours?" I asked.

"Business acquaintance."

Hot was right. The bright lights shined over sweaty bodies and gleamed over glasses held in the air. Two hundred people or more were crammed onto the dance floor, moving to the music. Tables on all sides, including a full balcony with a view over the entire club, surrounded the dancers. A man walked down the steps from upstairs, and I realized by the velvet rope it must have been a VIP area.

"Alex Reed, it's been too long." A handsome man in a suit shook Alex's hand and gave me a once-over. "I hope you brought me a present."

"Eyes up, Pedro. You're staring at my woman like she's your next meal."

"So sorry. So sorry." He put his hands up in surrender. "You have to admit, she is top of the line." He watched me curiously. "Tell the bartender to take care of you tonight. On the house. You're welcome to hang out upstairs if you'd rather. I'll come by and check on you." He walked toward the back of the building, and Alex guided me to a private table in the corner.

After a few drinks, I talked him into dancing with me. An hour or so later, we were drunk, sweaty, and way more touchy than we usually were in public. Alex grabbed another round, and I took a seat at our table to wait for him. The hair on my arms bristled as someone hovered over me. Pedro stood there, studying me.

"Can I help you?" I asked.

"What is it about you? Yes, you're a beautiful woman, but

beautiful women are everywhere. What is it about you that turns Alex into an overprotective love-sick puppy?"

"I'm not sure I would agree with that. Overprotective? Maybe. Love-sick? Hardly."

"I've watched you all night, trust me. I've never seen my friend this way about a woman. You intrigue me, Senorita." He walked away without another word.

Alex returned with a sour expression that was almost comical.

"What is wrong with you?" I asked.

He sat the shots down between us, grabbed one, and kicked it back. "Look gorgeous, I'm proud to call you mine. But if I have to threaten one more asshole that imagines you in his bed, then I'm going to actually kill someone."

I threw my shot back and leaned forward to whisper in his ear. "Maybe you could take me to your bed. You know, work out some of that aggression?" I could tell by Alex's hungry gaze that he was fond of my suggestion. He grabbed me by the hand and pulled me through the club.

We barely made it out to the limo before he was all over me. Pinned up against the car, I wrapped my arms around his neck as Alex ravaged my mouth. I reached to find the door handle so we could climb inside. He opened the door for us to get in, and we were finally alone. Closing the divider, he told the driver to take the long route home.

When we finally arrived back at the house, we were sweaty and exhausted. We showered quickly, then collapsed on the bed and drifted off to sleep without another word. My heavy eyes shut, and darkness closed in around me as fear and desperation took over my dreams.

* * *

MY HEART POUNDED hard against my chest and my breaths were shallow and weak. The effort I had given to escape was more than I ever thought I had in me. But, I wasn't sure I'd ever be able to get away. And I didn't want to think about what lied ahead for me if I didn't. I was too weak. Too cowardly.

Warm sticky blood dripped from my scalp, and I was lucky it wasn't worse. The last backhand I took was by far the worst. It knocked me sideways and into the corner of the wooden table. The bleeding hadn't stopped since.

The guy from the airport seethed. "Man, what is wrong with you? If they offer me less because she's injured, then it's coming out of your cut."

"Whatever. We have to get her under control, or they aren't going to want her anyway," the gravelly voice responded.

So here I sat, alone in this dark cabin, blood trickling from my head. The stench of copper, vomit, and urine was thick in the air. I wasn't even sure what point I urinated on myself. The shot they had given me had worn off, but I had no idea how long I'd been there or where we were going. How judgmental I'd been to say I was too smart to ever let anything like this happen to me.

Look how easy it had been for them to trap me.

It was a strange thing, thinking about what I had intended for my life and seeing how things played out. There's a sadness I had to wait out before I could make up my mind to do something about my situation. A mourning for the life I thought I would have. But looking back, that was when I made up my mind to do something about it. And I didn't care if it killed me trying. That was precisely what I planned to do.

The old man shuffled his way back into my cabin again and analyzed me as if he waited for my next move in a game of chess. His face, so well defined now, snarled in disgust at my appearance. The sun had not been kind to him, and it showed in his tough leathery skin and deep creviced eyes. The drab olive jacket hung off his shoulders, and he wore the old red toboggan that I had seen so often in my nightmares. Everything was so clear to me all of a sudden.

The only way they would take me was dead. If they sold me like they planned to, I'd wish I were. No matter what my weak self-esteem told me, I had something to fight for. Someone to fight for. And that thought alone was what made me stagger to my feet and stare him in the eye. If I had to, I'd jump overboard and face the grueling sea to escape these men.

A loud crack of thunder broke through the silence, and the shudder was felt throughout the boat.

Your grieving period is done, Liv.

The time has come to fight for Sophia. Fight for your daughter.

12

I remembered. Memories came flooding with intensity after the nightmare. I bolted for the bathroom and threw up before I reached the toilet. It was too much, and my stomach churned with the horrific knowledge.

These were not just dreams my conscience had conjured up, they were real. They happened, and I had to stop living in denial.

My name was Liv. I knew it with all of my heart, just like I knew my daughter was Sophia. I still couldn't see her face or features, but there wasn't a doubt in my mind.

Alex ran into the bathroom. "Jesus, Sophia! What the hell happened?"

"My name isn't Sophia."

"What?"

"My name is not Sophia!" I doubled over crying and couldn't catch my breath. Alex stepped around my mess on the floor and grabbed a washcloth from the sink. He squatted in front of me and tipped my chin toward him. Washing my face, he tried to calm me down.

"Sophia is my daughter," I said.

He paused, the realization evident in his eyes. "What did you say?"

"Sophia is my daughter. My name is Liv, and I think . . . I think I was supposed to be sold by traffickers." Tears ran down my cheeks, and Alex sat speechless on his heels, staring at me with a pale face and startled expression.

"I um. I need a minute," he said as he stood and left the room.

A few seconds after that, I heard my bedroom door open and close. He was in shock. I understood, but he should have tried being on my side of it. But, he just left me there alone, and I wasn't sure what to do next. I surveyed the bathroom floor and decided to clean it up and grab a shower.

When Alex returned, there wasn't any need to have a vomit-coated floor conversation. I found some cleaning supplies under the sink and began scrubbing the tile and marble. As I did, my insides turned when I recalled what just happened.

I had a daughter. And, she had been without her mother all this time. While I've been reading, shopping, and sailing the ocean, she had been trying to find me. Guilt consumed my mind. I should have been digging deep to figure out if I had a husband as well, but for some reason, my brain didn't even question it.

There was no doubt my heart belonged to Sophia and Alex alone. I stood under the hottest water I could tolerate and thought through my options.

Where did we live? How could I find her without a last name? I had to figure out how to reach her, but I also didn't want to lose what I had found with Alex. How would he cope with me having a daughter? We've never talked about having children.

I banged my forehead against the tile shower over and over. I couldn't believe it.

Liv. My name is Liv. Yes, that was right. My mother called me Livi. I grew up helping her in our family's flower shop, and snapdragons were her favorite. Sophia loved to stay with her on the weekends and played in the shop. I couldn't be sure, but I believed my father had passed. There weren't many memories of him surfacing, and the ones I had were from my childhood.

I remembered him reading to me as a child. He'd laugh as I asked for the same book every night—Rapunzel. I'd always wondered why I felt a connection to the story and why I clung to that memory while losing so many others. The revelation that small things were pushing themselves forward made me smile.

That's it. Keep going.

Then, another image, an old man coming toward me with leathery skin and an old greenish color jacket. I could see his face well enough to draw it now. Chills rolled over my skin, and my arms were heavy as if they were holding weights. This was too much for me.

Turning off the shower, I decided to step out before I collapsed. I needed to sit down and reflect so I could come to terms with all of this. But, what I really needed was to confide in someone. I had to get my thoughts and emotions out before they ate me alive. I considered calling Mary, but I needed to speak with Alex first. He was a substantial piece of my life, and this would involve him as well.

I wrapped myself in my robe and walked toward the window. I took in a deep breath and stared out at the deep, dark blue water. The waves were calm, and the water was soothing.

Something drew my attention toward the sand, and it took me a minute to realize it was Alex, sitting on the beach. Leaving him to his thoughts would probably be the right thing to do in this situation. But I didn't really feel like being honorable right then.

I needed support, and if he refused to talk to me, then that said multitudes about our future together. I reached for my shoes, but my temper caused me to miss, so I had to bend back down to snatch them again.

Smooth as always.

I slid them on as I stumbled out the door. How dare him! He just left me in that emotional state on the floor, so he could sit on the beach and sort through his confusion? His shock? He wasn't the one that forgot their own child. He definitely wasn't the one who was almost sold! By the time I made it out to the sand, still in my robe, I'd worked myself up into a frenzy.

Here comes crazy.

"How dare you! How dare you leave me alone up there! Do you have any idea what I am going through?" I yelled down the beach like a lunatic.

"Soph . . . I mean, um, listen to me, please." He stuttered. The man didn't even know what to call me.

"Listen to you? You should be listening to me. I'm dealing with all of this on my own, and you're supposed to be here for me!" I tried not to yell, really I did.

"I want to help you. No matter what that means for me, I want to do everything I can for you. I just needed to go somewhere quiet, so I could figure out what that is," he explained gently.

My steam ran out, and the build-up of tears came to the surface. I plopped down ungracefully beside Alex and took a deep breath. "I'm afraid of losing you."

His head jerked toward me. "You still want to be with me?"

"Why wouldn't I?"

He sat quietly for a few minutes. "I guess, I guess I just

figured if there's a child, then there must be a husband. Maybe you haven't remembered him yet. And even if there isn't a husband, you have a life somewhere. A family. That is hard for me to compete with."

"Alex, if I had a husband, there's no way I would have been able to give you such a large piece of my heart. There has never been a doubt in my mind about that. I want my daughter back, but I also want you."

"Is that really what you want? The happily ever after?" he asked.

"Yes. That's exactly what I want."

"Then that is what I'll give you, Liv."

We sat on the sand for what seemed like half the morning. It was a productive silence. Alex's lips pursed and his brow furrowed as if he contemplated a way to make it all work. I sat beside him, trying not to have an anxiety attack at the latest revelations. See? Productive.

Mary walked down the beach toward us, a look of concern on her pretty face.

"I think I'm going to head inside to work on a few things. I'll give you ladies a chance to talk."

"What's going on?" she asked, approaching us.

"What isn't going on is probably easier to answer." I patted the sand beside me. "Want to sit down?"

She bent down on her knees in front of me with a worried expression on her face.

"My name is Liv."

Her head jerked back like she'd been hit. "Liv? Your memories have returned?"

"Not all of them. But I remember the face of one of the men who took me. And I remember who Sophia is."

"So, who is Sophia then?"

"She's my daughter, Mary." My eyes filled up with tears, and I fell apart with my face in my hands. It was the first time

I had let the fear and relief roll through me all at once, and it was a lot to endure. Mary stayed by my side with her arm around my shoulders but never left my side. That was all I could ask from her right then.

"How old is she?" she asked.

"Close to your age. I still can't see her clearly. It almost feels like I've woken from a dream, and all of the details are still hazy. What if she blames me? Hates me? I'm so ashamed. If I could just remember the last of the missing pieces."

"It will come. And when it does, I'll be here for you."

* * *

LATER THAT EVENING, I sat in the armchair with nothing but the sound of waves echoing throughout the room. Mary invited me to eat dinner with her while Alex was occupied, but I didn't have an appetite. I had not eaten a bite all day. An unexpected knock on the door startled me.

I opened the door to Mary, and she glanced to her left and right before entering and shutting my door quickly behind her.

"Look, I can tell you from experience, you aren't as ninja-like as you think you are," I told her. "But, I appreciate your effort."

"I just need to speak with you in private. I could get fired for talking about the boss."

"What is it?"

"One of the maids overheard the kitchen staff whispering about an argument between Mr. Reed and Ian. Mr. Reed was accusing Ian of trying to jeopardize his relationship with you out of jealousy. Ian apparently said you should be with him and he saw you first on the boat that night when Mr. Reed jumped in to save you. He blamed him for ruining his chance with you."

"Wait, Ian was on the boat that saved me? This is the first I've heard about it."

Mary shrugged. "Honestly, they probably didn't think it was important. There are always several staff members on these overnight trips."

I thought back to the day the officials were on the island. The kitchen staff was huddled together, gossiping when I walked in. Was their argument what they were whispering about?

"What happened then?" I asked.

"Ian said he wouldn't stop fighting for you, then Mr. Reed hit him."

"He hit him?"

"Yes, ma'am. She said he hit him real good, and it took a few minutes for him to get back up. When he did, Mr. Reed said, 'I don't care who you were to my father. Don't push me.' Then he walked off."

"I know brothers can have horrible sibling rivalry, but this seems extreme." My teeth bit down into my lip while I considered everything she had said.

Mary's eyes were huge. "Brothers? What are you talking about?" she asked.

Oh, no.

"Mary, you can't say anything about this. You have to promise me."

"Of course I promise, but why haven't I heard this before?"

"I heard that Alex's father raped a staff member, and she had a baby. Anna said the child almost ruined everything, which leads me to believe he could have taken Alex's inheritance. With Ian being adopted, I just came to the conclusion that. . ."

"Ian is the bastard baby," she finished. "How did I not know about this? I mean, I know I keep to myself, but I do keep an ear out for gossip. I can only imagine how quiet this was kept."

"You have to promise me you will not say anything. Things are bad enough as it is."

"You have my word. I have to hurry back before Isabel realizes I'm gone."

"Mary, thanks again for everything."

She smiled and snuck back through the door.

Exhaustion filled every part of my body. The day crept by. It seemed as though a year had passed and I hadn't gotten anywhere. I dropped down on the bed and stared in a daze at the ceiling.

"You want me to come back later?" A voice asked. Alex leaned up against the doorway, observing me. "You seemed like you were in another world before I interrupted."

"No, I could use the distraction. What have you been up to?" A part of me wondered if he would mention Ian or try to protect me from anything that had to do with him.

"I may have a solution to our problem," he said. I stared at him expectantly. "I'm not sure where you live, but I think you were picked up in Miami, Florida. I did some research throughout the day. In May, a missing person's report was filed for someone named Olivia Brinkley. They said she disappeared from the Miami airport and never showed to meet her daughter, Sophia."

He stared at me as I processed the information. "Olivia Brinkley. That's right. But friends called me Liv."

"Liv?" He paused to make sure I was absorbing everything he said. "Sophia stated in her report that a gentleman came back to the airport for her. She told officials that he said he was supposed to pick her up and meet you. But, she refused to go with him. She said you would never send a stranger for her."

Tears streamed down my face. Good girl. Smart girl. "Okay. So now what?"

"I think we should go to Miami. Start there and see what we can find out. We can take the larger boat that you like to call a yacht, make a vacation out of it." He grinned. "Maybe we can find Sophia and sort things out. She may want to live here with us. You love the island, and this is where my home is. What do you think?"

Alex had a hopeful gleam in his eyes. He loved this place, but he wanted me in his life as well. "What if it doesn't end well? She may want to stay in Florida with her friends or stay with my mom. She could feel deserted by me. What then?"

"Let's just take it one step at a time, okay? If she doesn't want to move, we'll figure something out. But, she may just surprise you altogether."

It's challenging to deny Alex's optimistic expression, and my heart refused to do so. I worried about what would happen when we got there, but he was right. We had to do this.

"Let's go." I smiled.

13

I stumbled to my feet and stared at the old man in the face with defiance. He tilted his head to the side and said, "Don't even try it, little miss. You'll be dead before you make it to the door."

"Maybe I don't care anymore."

"Of course you do. I've seen your type before. Strong-willed, stubborn, and bold. Hell, I married one of em'. But this isn't the time for it. You're only gonna get yourself killed." He stepped closer, and I took a step back. "Plus, where do you think you're gonna go? We're in the middle of the sea."

I took in my surroundings and tried to come up with a plan. My head still pounded from hitting the table, and I hadn't been able to think clearly. They'd made sure there wasn't anything in the room I could use as a weapon. Besides some pieces of furniture, the place had been emptied. Why didn't I take that self-defense course with Tina?

All at once, the old man came at me. I turned to dodge him, but his grip tightened, and his filthy nails clawed into my skin. I jerked as hard as I could, but the action caused his nails to shred the skin on my arm. I pushed away and took off toward the door, but he jumped after me. Crashing hard to the floor, he grabbed hold of my ankles.

He pulled my body back into the room while I held onto the threshold of the door. I kicked as hard as I could to get away.

Fight Liv! Fight harder! One good kick to the face and the old man yelled out, releasing his hold on my ankle. There was my chance.

I took off running through the door and turned toward the opposite direction I went earlier. There had to be a weapon around there somewhere, right? I searched for anything I could get my hands on. The rain had made the deck slippery, and I struggled to see where I was going. All at once, I hit the railing at the front of the boat.

I turned to find a life preserver, float, or anything at that point. I had to get out of there. Lightning flashed, and a man stood right in front of me. It was the guy from the airport. I could make out his physique, but I still couldn't see his face clearly.

"Where do you think you're going to go? You would rather take your chances with the sharks? Olivia, I'm hurt."

"Please stay away from me. You can't do this. This is kidnapping."

"No, that's silly. There's no real money in kidnapping, sweetheart. This is trafficking, and we are making a fortune off of you. So, I'm not going to be very pleased if you mess this up for me. Do you understand?"

I stepped one foot on the railing, then the other.

"Olivia, get down. If you make this difficult, you're not going to like the consequences."

All at once, I turned on the railing and jumped. I didn't even think about it. I was vaguely aware of him grabbing for me, but he was too late. I hit the cold dark water and swam away from the boat as quickly as I could. I stayed underwater until my lungs screamed for air.

When I broke the surface, the boat was maybe forty to fifty feet away from me. A massive wave knocked me under right as I breathed in, and I swallowed a mouthful of saltwater. Fighting to the surface once more, I burst through the waves, gasping. Thunder roared over my head, and bright light from the boat glided over the water and shined across my face.

Swim harder.

I couldn't let them see me.

* * *

WHEN I WOKE from the nightmare, I didn't breathe hard or sweat. I was used to the disturbing dreams by then, and it wasn't information that I hadn't already figured out in my head. It was like the final pieces of the puzzle, and I was glad to have them. I never realized how much fight I had in me until that moment. It made me proud. And because of that, I would see Sophia again.

I climbed out of bed, and something caught my eye outside.

The docks were full of life. I looked out to see multiple staff members coming and going from a large, sleek, white boat. Alex must have had everyone preparing us for Miami. Excitement bubbled through me, but so did uncertainty.

What if Sophia had no interest in living there with us? She had her own life with family and friends we had to consider. Would Alex pick everything up and move to the states with us? I tried hard to not think about those details right then.

One step at a time, Liv. One step at a time.

I finished packing my suitcase and products from the

bathroom. I paused and walked toward the table beside the bed. After pulling the drawer open, I picked up my favorite novel and found the scrap paper tucked inside. Just like last time, it called to me.

I slipped it in my bag, knowing I was meant to take it with me. Lastly, I packed my shell that Alex and I found on the beach. The memory brought a smile to my face.

Isabel stopped by as I collected my things. For a while, she didn't say a word. Then she bit her bottom lip, trying not to cry. "Do you have everything you need? I can get you some extra luggage, or essentials. We don't want you leaving and wishing you had packed more.

I will just . . . I'll just go and. . ." Isabel put her hand over her mouth to cover the heart-wrenching sob. I never realized how much this would affect her.

"You know I'll probably be coming right back, don't you? There's no need to get all weepy on me now." I wrapped my arms around her.

"I'm so, so sorry. It's just that Alex is the closest thing I've ever had to a son, and I've always wanted a daughter. What if I never see you again? I'm not sure if my heart would survive it."

"You've been with Alex for a long time, haven't you?"

"Yes, Alex was just a child when William started sailing for Mr. Reed. They were going to hire a nanny to help Luciana anyway, so it seemed like a good opportunity for me. You see, I was never able to conceive. I always planned on having a large house full of children and, eventually, grandchildren. I'm not sure what happened, but I have to trust in God's plan that it wasn't meant to be." Her eyes shimmered with the tears she had probably held on to for years.

"The first time I saw Alex, his dark hair stood out in all directions, and he had chocolate and dirt smudges on his face. I fell in love immediately. He called me 'Izzy' until he was old enough for his father to reprimand him for it. I have to say, I loved that nickname," she smiled at the memory.

"Alex loves you, Isabel. You have to know how much you mean to him."

She grinned a sad smile and held a seriousness I had never seen in her eyes before. "Just promise me one thing. Whatever happens, remember what you have with Alex. Love is a rare gift, and we tend to find those gifts during the most unusual times in our life. That man would walk through fire for you. Don't give that up, okay?"

I watched this woman who had been there for me since I arrived. This selfless, sassy, and stern woman had a heart larger than the sea. "I love you, Isabel."

She came forward and wrapped her arms around me. "And I love you, child."

"You're not losing us forever. Even if we did move to the states, we would be back from time to time. You have my word."

I walked the gardens alone that afternoon, reflecting on the last couple of months and all that had transpired. I would be lying if I said that it had been stress-free. The events that brought me to the island were horrifying and disturbing. But Alex changed everything. He had rescued me from the wicked fate those men planned for me.

Some girls were not that lucky.

Then he protected me and even grew to care for me. I still prayed that the rest of my memories would return. I want to know how I ended up in a situation like that, but I also wanted to help others and prevent them from getting trapped by such evil individuals.

I stood on the cliff edge by the willow tree where I first had lunch with Alex. It was still my favorite spot, and I hoped I could show it to Sophia.

So many places I wanted to take her and people I

wanted her to meet. I wondered what she would think. Would she be upset at me for forgetting her? Guilt slowly slithered its way into my heart and squeezed, as I closed my eyes to battle the tears. After taking several deep breaths, I fought back the overwhelming anxiety, and it finally dissipated like a fog, while it awaited another opportunity to resurface.

Alex planned to leave at sunset, so I had a couple of hours before I needed to be at the dock. William offered to navigate for us, so Alex and I could relish some time together on the sail over.

We hadn't had a chance to really enjoy each other over the past couple of days. He had been slammed with making arrangements for our trip and tying up loose ends so he could be away from work. I looked forward to it more than he knew; I might have packed a few outfits just for him.

Ah yes . . . I couldn't wait to see those possessive green eyes.

A light breeze brushed across my face, and I closed my eyes at the coolness. Even if it was only a few days, I would miss this. I considered walking to the market to see Anna and Miguel, but that would be too much like a goodbye. These people were part of my family now; they had to know I'd return.

Saying goodbye to Mary would be the hardest. She arrived at my door, acting like she was going to a funeral. An overwhelming sadness consumed all other emotions, and I blurted out an idea before my mind caught up with my mouth. "Come with us." Her eyes met mine at my words, and she grinned while shaking her head back and forth.

"You know I can't do that."

"Why not? I can't think of a good reason for you to stay here. Besides, I need you."

"There's no place for me in the states, Liv. I'm just an uneducated servant, and this is all I'll ever know," she said.

"But your offer means more to me than I can put into words." She handed me a scrap of paper with writing on it.

"What is this?" I asked.

"My number. Alex bought me a phone. He said he knew you'd want to keep in touch with me while you're gone. I've never even used a phone before." She grinned like it was Christmas.

"You aren't an uneducated servant, Mary. You just haven't had the opportunity you deserve. I'm going to make sure you get it, you have my word." I gave her a lingering hug, then she walked with me down to the dock. I saw the yacht up ahead, but I stopped in my tracks at the sight of Alex's sailboat also secured there.

"Liv, what's wrong?" Mary asked.

I was speechless. I walked toward the boat and threw my hands over my face while tears filled my eyes. On the side of the boat, in elegant black writing, it said Liv. I glanced over toward the yacht, where Alex leaned on the rail watching me. He gave me a wink and started walking toward us.

"You like it?" he asked.

I threw myself at him, and he caught me, stepping back to keep his balance.

"It's beautiful. I can't believe you finally named your boat." I wiped the tears from my face and tried to compose myself.

He smiled at me with loving eyes and said, "I had to wait until inspiration hit." Lightly brushing his lips across mine, he asked, "Are you ready?"

"Just saying goodbye. I'll be right there, I promise."

Mary gave me one last hug. "Call me when you find out where Sophia is, okay? I want to know everything."

"You know I will."

Alex picked up my suitcase and nodded a goodbye to Mary. With one last wave, I followed him to the large boat that would take me home.

Alex said I could relax on the sun deck or in the main cabin where we would sleep. There were two cabins and a small kitchen area so we would have plenty of room for all of us.

"William is getting everything prepared in the engine room, and Ian is surveying the deck gear," Alex informed me. " I'll get us out of the harbor while they are doing the prep work. Then William will take over for me."

"I wasn't aware that Ian would be joining us," I said.

"I hadn't planned on it. I'll be straightforward with you, Liv, things have not been well between us lately. He says he wants to help. I think as much as he hates me, he has a soft spot for you. But, we had a little heart to heart, and he seems to be trying."

"By heart to heart, you mean a fist to the face?" I asked, grinning.

"Something like that." He smirked and bent down to kiss me. "Go explore, and I'll come to find you soon."

A rumble of excitement bubbled through me at the prospect of having Alex to myself for the next couple of days. The boat shuttered, and I realized he was pulling away from the dock. Before I climbed the ladder to the sundeck, I took one final glance at the house.

Straining my gaze toward the top of the cliff, I saw Mary huddled on the small bench that overlooked the sea. I'm almost positive she was crying. She stood and hurriedly walked inside the house without looking back. My heart hurt for her, and I planned to do anything I could to help.

I stood by the railing, letting the sun warm the ice-cold uncertainty that had settled in the pit of my stomach. To be so content and unsettled at the same time was difficult for the soul. I needed to feel secure and whole. Having Sophia and Alex, in my life at the same time, would hopefully do that. They were my family now, both of them.

I climbed up to the top deck and laid down in one of the loungers. My eyes shut against the bright sun, but the warmth soothed my tired body. A cool breeze blew off the ocean, and I said a silent thank-you for the beautiful weather.

The sun's rays were blocked at once, and I opened my eyes to see Ian standing over me. "Ian, Alex told me you were joining us. I really appreciate the help."

"Of course. I know I'm not always the easiest person to be around, but I want you to be happy. If I'm honest, I guess I had to get over a little bit of jealousy. I had my eyes set on you first, you know." He grinned.

"Thank you, Ian. I really appreciate your honesty. And I'm glad you're here."

"Thank you. I have some things to do, but I'll catch up with you later."

He left me to my solitude, and I attempted to get some rest. Ian didn't seem like a bad guy, I think his jealousy controlled his emotions. Did he know they were brothers? Would he hate him even more?

I couldn't relax right then. I finally decided to move around, plus, I was anxious to explore my temporary home. Climbing down from the sundeck, I opened the first door I came to. I discovered the tiny kitchen area at the beginning of my tour. The striking contrast from the bright white exterior to the dark shiny wood on the inside made the design beautiful and sophisticated.

Dark wood cabinets and black appliances screamed masculinity. A wooden dining booth sat in the corner with black leather bench seats. If Isabel had anything to do with it, I would put money on the refrigerator stocked with essentials.

Because my curiosity was too much to endure, I opened the fridge door to take a peek. Yes, Isabel had left her mark. I wasn't sure how she closed the door from all of the fruit, cheese, and wine. That was always her favorite thing to serve us, and I guessed it was her way of being romantic.

I resumed my tour of the boat, but the sun blinded me at every turn. If I could locate my luggage, I'd grab my sunglasses. The next cabin I arrived at had a sizable bed, big enough for two people, and my bags sat on the end. Bingo. I blindly dug around for my sunglasses at the bottom of my tote, and I finally had some luck. I had a sun deck to return to. Before I left, I checked things out around the cabin.

I knew the rooms wouldn't be massive, but it was still a bit of a shock compared to the house I was accustomed to. But I had everything I needed, and it was only temporary. A small dresser was situated across from the bed, but I left my clothes packed. It seemed more convenient since we wouldn't be aboard for long. Dark wood planks made up the walls and ceiling of the room, and a small table with a lantern barely fit beside the bed.

It was small, but Alex expected us to arrive in Miami in two days so it would work. I questioned why we didn't fly, but he said he would like a couple of extra days with me before we arrived.

I continued on and eventually found another door that had to be the second cabin. I knocked first, knowing we had other guests onboard. The knock was met with silence, so I slowly opened the door and peeked inside before barging in. This room had dark wood accents, just like the main cabin.

A small bunk sat on the far side of the space, and a small square table was parallel to the beds. A wooden dresser, similar to the other room, took up one wall on my right, and there wasn't much more than that. It was just the basics and not much to see, really. But something about this room was different. A dark sensation attached to a sense of déjà vu nearly took my breath away.

I turned to leave, and something caught my eye. The

wooden table in the center of the cabin called to me. I stood and stared at it for a minute, not wanting to walk back across the room, but the voice in the back of my mind would not leave me alone. I stepped closer and laid my hand down to trace the grain of the wood.

My mind pushed and pulled, but I was unable to piece together the puzzle. The putrid smell that hovered in the cabin turned my stomach, but also seemed vaguely familiar. I wasn't sure what had come over me, but I needed to get out of there.

"Well, it's about time we meet," an old voice sounded from the door. "Isabel told me that you were a pretty thing, and I have to say she's right."

That voice. I couldn't turn around. My entire body had seized up, and fear had taken over every nerve. I would know that gravelly voice anywhere. *Please, God, no.* My hand grazed the wooden table to the sharp corner at the end. Dark red stained the wood, and I slowly brought my hand up, recalling the scar on my scalp.

Oh no. No. No. No...

"Ma'am, are you alright?" His hand came down on my shoulder, and I spun ready to fight if needed. I would do anything to get away from this man. His hands came up to calm me down, "I'm not tryin to hurt ya. Just want to see if you're okay."

I looked up at the face I'd seen in my nightmares for weeks. The face that was brown and wrinkled from the sun. The man that wore the red hat, William. Isabel's William. "Don't you dare touch me," I said menacingly.

"I'm not touching you, ma'am, and I didn't mean to startle you. Maybe I should go get some help, okay? Just calm down."

"Calm down? Are you serious right now? How can you do

this? How can you do this to innocent women? And Isabel? What would she do if she knew what you are?"

The last thing I said struck a nerve, and his face changed immediately. This was the face I remembered. The snarled and ugly hate-filled expression, worn on the face of an old man who had no conscience.

"Now, you listen here, you little bitch. The only reason you're alive is because you put yourself on Alex's radar. You've been protected. Don't make a mistake, thinking I won't kill you if you threaten my honor with my wife. I protect what I love, and I don't care who's in the line of fire."

"Love? You don't know what love is. Someone who would do the things you do has no idea what the meaning of love is. I'll do everything in my power to free Isabel from your appalling and horrid existence!"

He made a grab for me, but I dodged him and bolted for the door. I needed to get help. I had to find Alex. I glanced back to see how far he was behind me, and I hit an unforgiving wall of muscle.

"Hey, are you okay?" Ian asked as he wrapped his arms around me.

"No. No, I'm not! William is my kidnapper. He's the one who drugged me, and we have to tell Alex. We need to have him arrested!"

"I've got you, okay? I won't let anything happen to you, you have to trust me." Ian's blue eyes turned into a slide show, flipping through my mind.

The airport, the dock, and the boat . . . He was there. He took me from the airport. All this time, the devil was living under the same roof. I jerked away from him, gasping. "You! You did this to me. I remember. I remember everything. We were drinking at the pub, and I was light-headed. You took me to that boat, didn't you? This boat. How can you do this? What kind of monster are you?"

His face changed to someone I didn't recognize, and he started to smile as he spoke, "Now Olivia, is this any way to speak to an old friend? We have been through a lot together, you know? And plus, you left the airport with me willingly, so don't forget that. Let's sit down to talk, and I'm sure we can come to an arrangement."

"An arrangement? You drugged me and kidnapped me! You were going to sell me," I screamed.

A creak from the door sounded, and every head in the room spun around. Alex stood there, staring at me with shock and anger. "What did you say?"

"I remember everything. Every horrifying detail," I said tearfully. I took a step toward Alex, but he dove through the air and landed on top of Ian, hitting him repeatedly. Ian wasn't even putting up a fight. I've never seen so much fury from one man, and it was frightening to behold.

"I will kill you," he shouted. "I will kill you both!" He continued beating Ian in the face, and blood coated Alex's fist. William huddled in the corner, not even trying to stop him. "I told you I wouldn't be a part of this! You swore to me that you weren't doing this anymore, and I trusted you. I refuse to be a part of your sick side job!"

Ian chuckled. A cackling, crazy belly laugh exploded from him while blood dripped from his mouth. He had gone insane. "You dumb shit. She never had a clue you knew anything about this until now. You screwed that up yourself." Ian spat blood to one side and laid back down. "Like you screw up everything else. Your father would be so proud."

Alex slowly turned toward me to gauge my reaction. He stood up steadily and calmly reached out for me.

"Liv, baby, it isn't what you think. I want you to listen to me, okay?"

"You knew? All this time, you knew they were the ones who took me?" A sharp crack sounded through the air, and I knew my heart had just shattered. I never in my wildest dreams thought that Alex would have anything to do with something so vile.

I couldn't have been that naïve and stupid, right? Had the truth been in my face the entire time, and people were laughing behind my back? People that I considered family.

"No! Please let me explain."

My throat tightened up, and I couldn't get a breath. Dizziness clouded my vision. My body limply slid down the wall as a sharp sting hit my arm. Please, God. Please protect me from these monsters.

"Why in the hell did you do that, William?" Alex shouted.

"She needs to calm down, and we need to talk," William answered.

14

My sleep-hazed brain tried to wake as I stretched my arms over my head. I didn't feel as comfortable as usual. I mean, the bed wasn't hard, but it didn't have anything on the luxurious mattress at the house.

I reached to the left of the bed where Alex usually slept, and the coldness of the sheet reminded me I was alone. I raised my head, and the view of the main cabin cleared the fog that protected my mind from the truth. The boat. I was on the boat.

William and Ian. They were the ones who took me. Took me from my daughter, and tried to sell me like a piece of property. My mind fought with my heart and told me this was all a bad dream, just like the others I'd had. But, I would never forget the look on Alex's face when he realized I knew their secret. How could any of this be real? It must have been a mistake, right? I sat up, jumping at the sound of a deep voice in the corner of the room.

"I'm sorry William sedated you," he said. "It did help with the anxiety attack, but I'm sorry nonetheless."

I stared at him but didn't reply. Words escaped me, and I

was afraid if I did speak, I would excuse him for something unforgivable. That was how messed up my heart and head were at that moment. Nothing made sense, and I tried to find a reason or excuse to do whatever I needed to do to stop the pain. It didn't matter if it was right or wrong when the heart was involved.

"Why did you save me from drowning? Is it because you almost lost a big paycheck? Is that the only reason?"

"No, of course not. You can't actually believe I had anything to do with this."

"Then, why?"

"We were sailing from Miami, and I had been in my cabin working all night. The storm hit, and I heard a commotion, so I went outside to see what happened. I caught a glimpse of your face when the lights skimmed over the waves, and I knew instantly that I had to save you. I just jumped in. William and Ian said they happened to find you when we were at sea. I had a feeling they were lying, but I wanted it to be true. So, I pushed the truth, the real truth, to the back of my mind because I wanted you. I knew we were meant to be together."

He continued, "You have to know I had nothing to do with you being taken away from Sophia. I truly thought you were Sophia, and I had no idea you had a daughter. It devastated me to find out a mother had been separated from her child. You know what I went through, and I would never do that to someone. This business was set up long before I took over, and when my father died, I put a stop to it. I should have turned them in for the things they did, but that would have ruined my father's company. I had just inherited a multi-million dollar industry, and I couldn't be held responsible for letting it fail."

"Why?"

He knew what I was asking. I didn't have to say anything

more than that. He sat in silence, unmoving. I wasn't sure if he refused to answer the question or didn't know the answer. But, I deserved a reply.

"Why?" I screamed. My throat burned from the effort.

"Liv, you have to understand these things happen all over the world every day. Am I supposed to protect every woman in the world from trafficking?"

"You've got to be kidding me. Do you think I'm stupid? They took me to your boat, Alex. This isn't about you failing to protect me. This is about your part in ruining women's and children's lives. What? Just because you weren't the one drugging and carrying them off means you're free of guilt? Is that what you've told yourself all these years?"

"You have no idea what you're talking about," he said with a warning in his voice.

"The morning my memories came back, we sat on the bathroom floor, and I told you I had been taken by human traffickers. I remember your startled expression, and you left me lying on the floor alone. You knew, didn't you? You knew it was them."

"I knew it was a possibility. I'd hoped I was wrong."

"Even Sophia's father had the decency to walk away from me when I was an eighteen-year-old new mother because he knew he would eventually hurt us. Until this point in my life, I thought that was the worst thing anyone has done to me. You lied to me, Alex. If you had a suspicion that I was in danger around Ian or William, I had a right to know."

"I would never let them harm you. You have to know that."

"Do I?"

He sat and stared at me for a long time as if he contemplated his next move. I wasn't sure why. There wasn't anything he could say to change the ending of our love story.

"I can't live without you. I love you."

"Get out, Alex."

Alex stood, stepping toward me, so I made myself more pronounced. "Get out now!"

He calmly backed toward the door. "I'm going to give you some time to think, and I'll be back to talk again." He left and closed the door behind him.

I laid on the bed, sobbing for hours. That was supposed to be a trip of celebration, reuniting with my daughter, and starting my life with Alex. Now what? I wasn't naïve enough to think these guys were going to let me go after I remembered what they did.

I would turn them in. They had me sheltered on that island, away from the real world, oblivious to everything. I should have investigated more after the man at the market recognized me. I knew. I knew in the pit of my stomach that something was off.

That's why the officers were at the house. That strange man, Herb. Did he call in a report? It all made sense now. But, why did Alex give me the information he'd researched with my full name and where I was taken? I analyzed every moment, every comment, and there's so much I didn't understand. Something inside me said it was because he genuinely didn't know the whole story.

Ian and William could have been hiding this from him, angry that Alex put a stop to it after his father died. But Alex never turned them in. Never made them pay for what they did. That was his part in everything. Even so, how could someone heal after this? How could I explain to my heart that this deep-seated trust came from a place of manipulation? An ache across my chest forced me to lie back down. How would I get myself out of this situation?

The door opened and I sat up quickly on guard. It wasn't Alex that frightened me. William and Ian were still on board, and I knew what they were capable of.

"It's just me, Liv," Alex said. "William and Ian were dropped off at the house. I need some time alone with you."

"What? You just dropped two criminals off? Did you even call the police, Alex?"

His silence told me everything I needed to know. Somewhere in the back of his mind, he knew the trafficking was still happening. Pretending it wasn't, doesn't change things.

"Take me to Miami. Now."

"We will, but first, we have some things to work through, and I need some time alone with you to do that."

"What do you want from me?" I asked.

"What I've always wanted since the moment I laid eyes on you. I want you."

"You understand that will never happen now, right?"

He stared straight ahead at me like he was waiting for an explanation.

"You told me I could trust you, Alex. I gave you my whole heart without a second thought. You've been lying to me this whole time. How do you ever expect me to live with you knowing the things you've overlooked? The moment you suspected them, you should have told me the truth. Do you think I want you around my daughter?"

"And, there's nothing I can do to change your mind?"

"No, Alex. There's not."

"You have to know that if I could change things I would. I would do anything for you." He stood to leave without a second glance.

Before he made it out the door, I called out. "Where are you taking me?"

"I'm taking you to a place of reflection, Olivia. You need some time to think about what you're throwing away." He turned back one more time with tears in his eyes, then walked out of the room.

I ran after him, slamming my fist on the door and yelling

his name. It was no use. The door was locked, and he was gone. I threw myself on the bed with my hands over my face.

What could I do now? I needed to get to Miami, to Sophia. I didn't know how long I laid there crying, but eventually, my body crashed, and I fell asleep.

* * *

WHEN I WOKE AGAIN, the boat shuddered as it came to a stop. I stretched to look out the window of the cabin, and I could barely see sand and trees that made up a small island. I had no idea where we were.

My door opened, and Alex picked up my suitcases. "Alright, we're here."

"Where exactly are we, Alex?"

He continued walking out the door and toward the dock without replying. He turned abruptly and silently questioned if I was coming. I followed him blindly, as usual. It's not like I had any other options at that point.

From the dock, Alex led me to a trail through the thick green trees. I wasn't certain how long we walked, but with all of the twists and turns, it would be difficult to find my way back. Something told me that was the whole purpose. I took notice of each turn and unique change in the path in case I could get away. I wanted to be able to find my way out of there.

We finally came upon a small clearing in the middle of the forest. A cabin, no bigger than my bedroom, sat in the center. This place had been kept up quite well for it to be out in the middle of nowhere.

A small flourishing garden grew to the right of the house, and a natural stream ran to the left. Flowers decorated the front of the cabin, and two rocking chairs sat empty on the porch. It was quite charming. A screen door creaked open, and I glanced up.

"It's not the first of the month, what's the occasion?" A strange voice called from the front.

"Hello to you too, Mother," Alex called out.

Mother? You have to be kidding me.

His mom was supposed to be dead. Anna told me she was never found. The realization of how much he had hidden from me was like a knife to my chest.

"Any other secrets you would like to confess, Alex?" I asked with disdain.

One brow raised, his expression was not amused.

I'm not amused either.

"This is my friend, Olivia." He nodded his head toward my direction. "I thought I would introduce her to the island."

His mom's eyes cut to me briefly, and a trace of sympathy rose in them before she glanced back at her son with contempt.

"Well, I'm assuming you didn't bring her to meet your mother," she said while turning toward me. "So, I guess welcome to your prison is in order." She turned around and went inside.

We followed her through the front door where two chairs and a table took up the small living area and opened up to a tiny kitchen. The walls and ceiling were planked, with home-made wicker furniture throughout. Her house had a warm, almost southern appeal.

"What do you want from me?" she asked plainly.

"I think it might be good for Liv to have some time to reflect. Clear her head for a bit."

Alex's mother burst out laughing. I'm glad she thought it was funny. Alex patiently waited for her episode to pass before he said any more. She managed to compose herself, then stood in front of him with a snarky look on her face.

"Like father, like son, huh?" She turned to me when she spoke. "What did you do, little one? Did you try to leave him? They don't accept that easily, I can tell you from experience."

"Mother, that's enough," Alex demanded. He turned to me. "This is my mother, Luciana. You will be staying with her for a little while so I can fix this mess."

He dropped my luggage and turned to leave. I followed him out and tried to pull on his arm, begging him to listen.

"You can't be serious, Alex. You can't treat me like a prisoner!"

Alex kept walking away, so I took off running to get in front of him. I wanted him to look me in the eyes. Shoving him as hard as I could, I screamed in his face. "Look at me, Alex! Look at me!"

He lowered his gaze, and I could see the struggle behind his beautiful green eyes.

"Is this really what you want? To keep me imprisoned here and visit me once a month? This isn't a life for anyone, especially for the woman you love."

"Do you think I really want this? I want you with me everyday, waking up beside me! I've already told you that I will not go on without you. But you keep insisting that it's over. I have to show you, Liv. I have to show you that we are supposed to be together. Let me fix this. I can right this wrong. Just take some time to think about things, and you may feel differently by the time I come back." He walked around me without looking back.

"Alex, please don't leave me here. Please! Please don't do this to me!" I screamed.

"I don't have a choice, Olivia!" The rage in his voice reverberated throughout the air, and it was so intense I had to take a step back. Suddenly, a pair of hands rested on my shoulders, and they turned me toward the cabin. Luciana guided me back toward the porch, attempting to calm me.

"Come, dear. We have much to talk about," Luciana said.

As we walked back into the cabin, a high-pitched whistling from a kettle begged for Luciana's attention.

"Please sit here, dear. I'll fetch us some tea." Luciana stepped toward the small kitchen area, and I couldn't help but notice how she seemed to gracefully float as she walked. A tiny woman, her hair black as the night. I couldn't imagine how beautiful she was when she was younger.

"It's amazing what you can do with just some herbs and wildflowers," she said as she handed me a cup of tea.

I took a small sip and my eyes widened in surprise. The sweet earthy flavors warmed me from the inside out.

"This is wonderful, thank you." I took another sip and drew in a deep breath. "Where are we?"

"It's a private island around twenty miles from San Alder, and it's owned by the Reed family. They never officially named it, so I like to call it Isle Luciana," she joked.

I stared, blank faced.

"Are you alright?" she asked.

I wasn't entirely sure how to answer her question, so I didn't say anything. She nodded as though she could read my mind. Standing up, she patted me on the shoulder, then walked out to sit on the porch, giving me time to process.

I sat in the small cabin, trying to wrap my mind around the awful truth I had discovered. How could Alex do this to me? All this time, how did I not know? Sitting in the tightly enclosed space, I couldn't get a deep breath. I followed Luciana to the front porch and sat in the rocking chair beside her.

"I'm not alright. At this point, I'm not sure I'll ever be alright again," I admitted.

"Tell me. How did you meet Alex?" she asked.

"Would you like the long or the short version?"

"How about a short version with all of the important details."

I nodded my head in agreement. "I was drugged and taken by human traffickers." Luciana tensed and visibly swallowed. I gave her the highlights of all that had happened since Alex pulled me from the ocean. And after I finished, I looked up at her with tears streaming down my cheeks.

"He took care of me. We fell for each other, and by the time my memories came back, I—" I bowed my head in tears, ashamed of my next words. The truth that had been the hardest to come to terms with sat on the edge of my lips, and I couldn't find the courage to admit it.

"You're in love with him. You're in love with Alex, and no matter what he has done, that doesn't go away overnight, young one." Luciana watched me with knowing sympathy. She had the most beautiful green eyes. Eyes that were so familiar.

"You don't think I'm weak?" I asked.

"I don't know you well, but I do know you're far from weak," she said kindly. "So now that you know, Alex refuses to let you leave him. Is that correct?"

"Yes, that is right," I responded. "Luciana, I have a daughter. I have to get back to her."

Luciana relaxed back in her chair and took a sip of tea. "You know, the Reed family has been funding trafficking for many years. Of course, I wasn't aware of this until Alexander was a teenager. I was mortified, Olivia. I can't imagine anything worse in the world than to be sold as a slave and used for whatever purpose these psychotic men have in store. These were innocent lives, and I refused to be a part of it. So, I told my husband I planned to leave and take Alex with me."

She sighed. "We fought, of course. He told me that he had never taken an innocent life and that it was all William. He was the one who sold these women and children like cattle. But who supplied the boats? The sedation that knocked them out? There's a reason the Reed family started manufacturing sedation medications, my sweet girl."

Luciana's next words rocked me to my core. "Standing by while lives are being destroyed is no different than holding that syringe yourself. And that, my angel, is what we have refused to have on our conscience when we die."

The realization hit me like a freight train. I looked at Luciana as if I stared at myself years down the road. This beautiful soul had been through hell with the love of her life, and she was strong enough to hold tight to her beliefs.

That's what I had to do. I would never look at Alex in the same light again, and I would never forgive him. I loved him, but the halo had disappeared. How would I make him see that he had to let me go?

"Anna told me you took a boat and left them both, but the boat was lost at sea."

"Yes, that sounds like something my husband would tell people. Too much money was at stake, and he could not risk the truth getting out. The day I left, I was brought here and dumped off without a way to contact anyone or escape. I tried once, and nearly drowned. I've spent most of my life here without another soul, except one day each month when he sends someone to make sure I'm still alive. Sometimes Alex brings me food or clothes from the market. But, I can take care of myself. I don't need any of them."

"This isn't living, Luciana. You've been cheated out of your life all for the sake of money."

"What life could there possibly be for me now? I have been here for over eighteen years."

"Who could leave their own wife or mother trapped like this for eighteen years?"

"I don't blame Alex. His father was the one who did this

when Alex was just a boy. He twisted and warped the details so that Alex grew up seeing a different version of it. Because he never had a part in the kidnappings or saw the women being taken, it wasn't of his concern. But, he never complained when his commission came in either."

"Alex could free you now that your husband is dead. Right?"

"He's never brought it up. And I know he is afraid of the business his father built crumbling in his wake. He doesn't want to be responsible for that."

"It appears he has the morals of his father, then," I admitted, harshly.

"How do you mean?" she asked.

"The accusations of rape. Anna told me about the bastard child that had been conceived after you left."

"I wish I could tell you what happened, but I was already gone at that point. My husband would sit and talk to me when he came to visit. Obviously, this wasn't a conversation I wanted to have with him, so I didn't push for details. But, I knew a child had been born, yes. But, don't ever confuse Alex's weak and distorted mindset for the cruelty that was his father. One was natural, and the other was taught. Alex never had the stomach for any of this. He despised it."

"Alex may not have inherited his father's demented nature, but his brother is the epitome of evil," I said.

"I'm sorry?" she asked.

"His brother, Ian. He is the one who kidnapped me from the airport. I can't imagine the horrible things he and William have done to so many innocent lives."

"Olivia, what makes you think Ian is Alex's brother?"

"Well, I was told the gardener had raised him, and no one mentions his biological parents. He and Alex have a very competitive relationship, always at each other's throat. It just makes sense, I guess."

"Darling, Ian isn't Alex's brother. His father was a farmer that owed money to my husband. The farmer came up missing after a visit from debt collectors, and they brought Ian back to work off his father's debts. Such a sad situation and my husband felt guilty when he saw the boy. His mother had abandoned him years before. He said he would always make sure he had a place to live and work. Probably guilt over what they did to his father. He made Alex promise to do the same."

"But, what about the child? Did they get rid of it?"

"No. From what I understand, the girl still lives there."

"The girl?" I asked. My stomach clenched, and I sat my cup on the table before I dropped it. Could it really be? All this time, and I never figured it out?

"I believe her name is Mary, after Maria, her mother. My husband was quite taken with Mary. He had been quite proud to have a daughter, and he seemed to have a soft spot for her. But, I'm not sure what happened to her mother. He may have gotten rid of her like he does anyone else that gets in his way."

"I can't believe I never realized it. Mary is a saint, Luciana. She is the most trusted friend I have. She is completely unaware that he was her father. If she had known, she would have told me."

"Such a tragic life for a young girl," she replied.

"Tragic isn't the word for it, she deserves so much more."

* * *

Luciana showed me around the cabin and where I would sleep while I was there. There was a loft above the kitchen with a small bed and table. It was simple but comfortable. How long would he leave me there?

I had to use my time to forge a plan, but it was difficult to form a coherent thought. I couldn't see him releasing me, and spending the next eighteen years of my life in that cabin wasn't an option.

We ate a light dinner of vegetables from Luciana's garden and decided to turn in. It had been a long day, and the burden of what this family had done over the years weighed heavily on my mind. I laid in bed, awake with visions of young girls going through what I went through, and I was unable to quiet the sobs that wracked my body.

Alex had told me the report stated they had come back for Sophia. They had tried to take my baby girl. The thought of her going through what I had brought me more terror than I had ever experienced firsthand.

You could do whatever you want with me, but don't touch my child.

I couldn't fathom Alex having any part to play in the plans for taking my daughter. After all the lies, I didn't feel like he was capable of that. I had to find a way off that island, Sophia needed me. I would swim if I had to.

I laid in bed for half the night, tossing and flipping from side to side, restless and unable to shut my mind off. Most of all, I was afraid. The thought brought tears to my eyes once again, and once it started, it wouldn't stop. Scared I would end up like Luciana and terrified I'd never see Sophia again.

15

The next morning, I woke alone in the quiet house. I found some clothes in my luggage to throw on, and I came across the conch shell at the top of my bathroom bag. It seemed like a lifetime ago. Sadness tried to creep its way in before I forced it back down. Even still, I placed the shell on my bedside table. Seeing it reminded me of happier times. There were a lot of those with Alex.

I found Luciana in the garden working. I couldn't figure out what she was doing, though. No weed or dry plant in sight. She kept it in pristine condition, but I guessed she didn't have much else to do. "Can I do something to help?"

"Sure, how much do you know about gardening?" she asked.

"Not much, but I do remember helping my mom with her flowers and herbs."

"Perfect, can you to cut some herbs? Afterward, we'll hang them to dry from the porch. There are some clippers and twine in the shed if you can grab those."

We kept ourselves busy throughout the day, and I learned so much from her. A dark part of me said she taught me those things in case I'd be there for the next twenty years. I couldn't let that happen.

After lunch, we walked down to the beach, fishing poles in hand. She was either a natural at this, or she had a lot of practice. Every time I touched the pole, the fish would stop biting. It's like they knew a stranger was there. But, Luciana caught three fish quickly, and we sat on the porch while she cleaned them.

"How did you meet Alex's father?"

"He came to the island looking for a second location and cheaper labor for his company. He was a businessman through and through, it always seemed to be about the dollar."

"So, you grew up here?"

"Yes, I did. My parents were farmers. Anna was my childhood friend, actually. That is what baffled me when you said she believes I abandoned Alex. She should know me better than that."

"Anna seems to care a lot about him. They both do. It sounds as though she tried to step in and help when you left."

"I'm thankful. They never had children of their own, but she always wanted them."

"I'm sorry, Luciana. I'm so sorry for all you've been through," I offered.

"Don't feel sorry for me. Pray for all of the other lives they've ruined over the years." She paused from cleaning the fish. "Living like this alone is nothing compared to what they've gone through."

Luciana cooked the fish over a small fire outside, and I had to say, it was better than anything I had ever ordered in a restaurant. Fresh and seasoned with lemon and herbs from the garden, this woman knew how to cook.

Afterward, we sat on the porch in silence, and my thoughts drifted to Alex. What was he doing? When would he be coming back? Should I lie and say I would never leave him so I could get off that island?

I hated the part of me that wanted to say yes to him. The part that wanted him to never leave me. But, I could never live with myself, and I would never trust him. Alex had problems, and they started years before I came into his life. It was going to take a lot more than me to help him.

Lying in bed that night, I knew there would be no point in trying to sleep. Shutting my mind off was futile, and my body was restless. As quietly as possible, I crept down the small ladder from the loft, trying to keep from waking Luciana.

"Can't sleep?" she asked.

I jumped and let out a high-pitched yelp before I realized she sat in one of the chairs in the living area.

"Sorry, I didn't mean to frighten you."

"No, that's okay. I'm just too restless to lie down. You can only count the knots in the ceiling so many times before you start questioning your sanity."

"How many?" she asked.

"Twenty-eight," I answered honestly.

She smirked at my answer. "Did you know I have thirty-three wooden planks on my ceiling?"

The comment made me realize how much this life had affected both of us. The only difference was that she had been stuck in it for over eighteen years. We weren't built for their world, either one of us.

"Luciana, when did you know it was time for you to leave? I know you said you left when you found out what he had been doing, but was it right then, or did it take you some time?"

She stared without looking at me, in a world of her own. I wasn't sure what went through her mind, but when a tear rolled down her cheek, I knew Luciana had gone to a dark place.

"I'll never forget the night I learned the horrid truth. I only found out because it was an abduction gone wrong, similar to yours. The girl located a kitchen knife, and she stabbed William in the gut. They were closer to home than anywhere else, so they docked there to bandage his wounds. I saw the boat come in from the window and wanted to surprise Richard by meeting him out there."

"When I stepped on board, there was blood everywhere. Instantly nauseous and shocked, I remember my whole body shaking uncontrollably." More tears filled her eyes, and her voice shook with emotion. "I found them in the guest cabin, and the girl laid there lifeless. Richard tried to make up an excuse, but I knew what they were doing, and he eventually came clean. William told Isabel that he had a fishing accident. And I said nothing. For weeks, I didn't say anything until I could come to terms with what I needed to do. It was a long grieving process."

"That is so horrible. I can't imagine how you felt."

"Yes. It was awful. But, I guess the answer to your question is that I knew it was time for me to leave when I could no longer look at myself in the mirror. That's when I knew."

I stared at her, nodding that I understood what she meant. If I stayed with someone like him, I would not be able to look at myself every morning, either.

"Honestly dear, I felt like a trapped bird. I knew if I didn't free myself, I would die there."

"What did you say?"

"You mean about the bird? I felt trapped, and I needed to feel free."

I jumped up and climbed the ladder to my loft.

"Liv, where are you going, dear?"

I came down and handed her the book I held close to my

heart since arriving. Now I knew who the initials LR belonged to.

"Where did you find this?"

"It was in my nightstand. I can't tell you how many times I've read it, or how often I've looked at your handwriting."

She opened the book, and the scrap of paper fell out. Picking it up with one hand and the other over her mouth, she continued to cry.

Like a bird that used to fly,

Trapped in a cage, left here to die.

Will I ever see the sun again?

Or will this darkness do me in?

LR

"Sometimes, this book is the only thing that got me through the day," she admitted.

"Thank you. Thank you for writing that and for leaving it for me to find. Sometimes, it got me through the day as well."

She smiled and shook off the last of her breakdown. "Would you like for me to get you something to drink?"

"No, thank you. I appreciate it, but I may step outside for some fresh air before I try to sleep."

"It's a beautiful night out. Sometimes fresh air brings clarity and wisdom. See you in the morning, Olivia." She stood and walked to her bedroom.

I stepped out the front door and sat in the old wooden rocker on the porch. I could barely hear the waves, but it was enough to seep into my mind like tendrils and forced me to relax. I had a different perspective since speaking with Luciana. She had shed light on so many questions burning through my brain since yesterday, and I had gained strength and knowledge from her past experiences, as horrible as they were.

A soft rustling through the trees pulled my attention to the side of the house. I sat very still, hoping that a small animal had gone on its way to leave me to my solitude. I told myself I didn't hear anything, but the hair stood straight up on my arms. Something was wrong.

Someone was there. I stood and quietly stepped to the far side of the porch, watching and waiting. The sound of a bird called out through the night, and the breaking of the waves in the distance was all I could hear. The entire situation had me paranoid and freaked out. No one was on that island except Luciana and I.

Just go back to bed Olivia so you will stop imagining things.

As I turned to go back inside, firm pressure hit my ankles, and my legs went out from under me; my chest and face caught all of my body weight on the porch's wooden surface. Then, my torso was pulled across the wooden planks. Someone had a fierce grip on my ankles, dragging me toward them.

I clawed against the floor of the porch, but it was no use. My strength didn't even come close to matching theirs. I opened my mouth to scream, and a hand came down, smothering my cry.

"I would suggest you learn from your past mistakes and be a good girl for me," Ian whispered. "We have some things to talk about, and we don't want Luciana getting hurt, now do we?"

I shook my head, no.

"Good girl." Ian forced me out into the forest, leading me toward the beam of a flashlight in the distance. The air felt humid, and my clothes stuck to my skin, my breathing labored from adrenaline, as I struggled to keep his pace. He jerked me by my upper arm so I would keep up.

"It's about time. Don't have all night, Ian," William growled.

Ian shoved me down in the sand between the two men, and William pointed a gun at my head. They would never let me go. The first thing I would have done when I made it to Miami was turn them in, and they knew it.

I looked over at Ian. "I thought we had some things to talk about?" I asked.

"Oh, we do. But, we will do it with a revolver. You see, I'm not much on conversation." He smiled a psychotic eager grin, and his anticipation hummed through the air. He was that insane. Fear crept up my throat, and I wasn't sure if I could speak. I pushed forward in an attempt to keep them talking, but there was no way I could keep the tears from showing my vulnerable and weak position.

"Why? Why do you need to do this? Do you not think you've put me through enough?"

"You? Why is it always about you?" Have you ever had a thought in your pretty little head about anyone else? You don't know pain until you're a seven-year-old boy watching a strange man put a gun to your father's head and pull the trigger. And for what? Two hundred dollars. That's it. So, do not tell me how hard your life has been! You don't know pain!" Ian paced in front of me, attempting to calm himself. He let his control slip, and now he tried to regain his composure.

"The Reed family has done nothing but ruin my life, so forgive me if I don't mind taking a little something from the golden boy." He spat toward the ground and stood in front of my face. "The word is, he is searching for us right now. I guess he thinks a little retaliation will solve his problems. So, we decided to fix our issue with you first."

He stood directly in front of me. "Let's be blunt with each other, Liv. You're going to turn us in as soon as Alex liberates you from this island. And, we both know, lover boy will do that sooner rather than later. It isn't a chance we are willing to take, sweetheart," Ian said with certainty.

"Can we get on with this? Isabel has my supper waiting."

"Yeah, go ahead. I have a bag and heavy weights in the boat. We can dump her on our way back."

"When did you have time to pack that?" William asked.

"I already had it packed in the speed boat from the night she refused to drown at the dock," Ian replied, annoyed.

It was Ian. Ian tried to drown me at the dock that night. The bastard even carried me to my room afterward. The thought made chills run up my spine.

William lifted the gun to my forehead for a clean shot. Not one bit of guilt or doubt in his eyes as he looked at me. No conscience whatsoever. How many young women had he looked at with the same vile expression? I hoped Sophia knew how much I loved her and how hard I'd fought.

I prayed for protection over her, so she'd never know the desperation I felt right then. A loud crack split the silence in the night, and I was thrown back against the sand forcefully with the heavy weight of William on my chest.

I looked up into the same vile eyes that stared me down seconds ago, but now those eyes were fading. I screamed and shoved William's limp body off of me and scooted backward away from him. The black stain on his back grew larger and larger, but I continued to stare in shock, not quite believing he was gone.

I looked up to see Mary, crying and shaking, as she held the gun and stared at the corpse with disbelieving eyes. Ian took the opportunity to rush her, and her petite frame fell to the ground underneath his larger, stronger body, fighting for the gun.

I forced myself to break out of my frozen haze and snatch up the revolver William had intended for me moments before. Ian had seized the weapon from Mary and turned it around to her abdomen when I fired the gun. It wasn't a clean shot, but it was enough to distract him. My biggest fear was hurting her, so I was willing to take anything I could get.

Ian grabbed his shoulder and yelled in pain. When he turned around to face me, I shot again. The bullet went straight into the left side of his chest, and he collapsed to his knees. Ian reached toward us as if to make one last effort, then he fell forward, unmoving. It was over. I ran over to Mary and helped her up from the sand.

"Are you hurt? Did he hurt you at all? I need to know if you are . . . if you . . ." I grabbed her in my arms, and I was inconsolable. This crazy, stupid girl just saved my life again.

"Liv, I'm okay. Look at me. I'm okay. We saved each other." Mary's sweet voice broke through my state of shock.

"How? How did you find me?" I asked.

"Alex's boat came back that evening without you, and I knew something was wrong. I stayed on the bench out on the cliff all day watching for some kind of sign. Eventually, William and Ian showed up to take a speedboat, so I followed them. I grabbed the gun from Alex's sailboat before I left, I don't know why."

"I'm so thankful you did."

"Me too."

"Mary, we have to get out of here. We can take their boat, but we have to leave now before it is too late."

"We? Liv, this is my home. I don't know anything else," she said sadly.

"You have a chance to start a new life. I'll help you. You have to trust me, okay? Just please come with me," I begged.

Mary looked around her like she was taking in one final memory of the salty water and white sand. "Okay, Liv. I'm coming with you."

"We have to get to Luciana. We have to get her off this island."

"Who?"

"Alex's mom."

"What did you say?" Mary stopped in her tracks, shocked at my words.

"Mary, I have so much to tell you. But we're going to have to do it later. Come quickly."

We ran back to where the cabin was nestled in the trees. I questioned my navigating skills until we crossed the small stream, and I knew it would take me right where I needed to go if I followed it. The cabin came into view, and Luciana stood on the front porch looking out toward the tree line.

"Dear heavens, child. I've been worried sick. Something that sounded like gunshots woke me from a deep sleep, and I couldn't find you. Are you all right?" She finally noticed someone else was with me, and confusion crossed her face. "Who are you?"

"Luciana, this is Mary. I don't have time to explain, but William and Ian are dead on the beach. We have to leave immediately. Go get your stuff quickly."

"Well, Olivia. I can't just leave. Who would tend my garden? I have to make sure the weeds are pulled, and it's almost time to harvest the corn." She stared down at her plants on the porch, nervously fiddling with the leaves. "And these poor things demand some water, see?"

It hit me. It hit me hard.

She couldn't leave. She had lived there longer than anywhere else, and she was scared. I got nose to nose with her and grabbed her hands, demanding her attention. "Luciana, we have to leave now. This may be my only chance to get back to Sophia. I don't want to leave you here, but I won't force you to go. Do you understand?"

She took a few moments to consider everything I had said.

She placed both hands on my face when she softly spoke. "Take the boat north to the main island, San Brilee, where police headquarters is stationed. Tell them everything,

Olivia, and they will help you get home." She kissed me on the forehead and whispered. "In another life, I would have been proud to have you as a daughter-in-law."

She turned away to head back in her cabin. Her reply was absolute, and this was what she wanted. I stared in her direction long after the door closed.

"Liv, we have to go now." Mary snapped me from my daze.

We headed back the direction we came. The boat must have been secured to the dock at the shoreline; I hoped we could find it. We tried our best to follow the sound of the waves, but it took longer than I would have liked. Eventually, we broke through the tree line, and the ocean waves washed up at our feet. The dock was probably a couple of hundred feet from where we came out. We ran halfway to the boat, and I stopped in my tracks.

"What's wrong?" Mary asked.

"There are three boats. Why are there three docked?"

"I followed them in one, but there were only two, including mine when I arrived."

We slowed our pace, keeping a watchful eye on our surroundings. He was there. I could sense his eyes on me.

"Mary, I want you to run to the boat and get it ready to leave, okay?"

"What's going on?" she asked nervously.

"Alex is here." Mary's eyes were sympathetic, knowing he would never let me leave. We had to be ready. "Do you still have your gun?"

"Yes, I'll be close," she responded.

She ran toward the dock, and I stayed perfectly still on the sand. I slowly turned toward the island, and there he was. He was so handsome, sometimes I forgot.

"You know you shouldn't look at me that way, Liv."

I couldn't help it. He was still the most attractive man I had ever laid eyes on.

"Alex, you need to let me go. I think we both know that this thing between us has no future." As I said the words, sadness threatened to cripple me. I loved this man, and I didn't know how to shut off that part of my heart. Only time could do that.

"I can't do that. We belong together, and you know it as well as I do."

"William and Ian are dead, Alex. We shot them."

"I don't blame you, Liv. You were just protecting yourself. If I had gotten to them first, I would have pulled the trigger. I can fix this, and nobody has to find out about it. You know I'll take care of you. *You can trust me*," he pleaded.

"I'm sorry, Alex. I'm going home to Sophia, my daughter, and I need you to let me."

He stepped toward me, and I took a couple of steps back, stumbling. He reached for me and jerked me into his arms. The heat from his beautiful intense gaze fixed on my mouth before he possessed it with his own. The kiss was all passion, anger, and desperation. I had never had this with anyone before, but it didn't take the pain away. It never would.

I pushed away from him and tried to be firm. "Goodbye, Alex."

He watched me turn and walk toward Mary, out of his life forever. A click pierced the night air. I froze and slowly turned toward him. He had the gun pointed toward me, and his hands were shaking.

"Don't make me do this, Liv. I've already told you I can't live without you. You know we are meant to be together. You just have to look past all of this to see it. I love you, and I know you love me. You have to look past it. You know I'm right!" His hands shook. Sweat dripped down from his face, and dark rings rimmed his eyes.

Alex wasn't well.

"Look over it? Look over all of the lies told and lives lost? I'm not that person, Alex, and you wouldn't love me if I was." I took small steps toward the gun. He looked in my eyes with a mixture of determination, love, and anger.

I walked closer, and he slowly lowered the gun down by his side. I ran my hands down the sides of his neck, pulling him toward me, and kissed him one last time.

When I finally pulled back, I looked him in the eyes. "I love you, Alex, but I want to live a free and happy life. I don't want to spend my existence hiding secrets or face the possibility of being stranded on an island for eighteen years. You carry a part of Luciana in you, and that is who I fell in love with. The tender, loyal, beautiful soul that would do anything for the woman he loves. Yet you also carry a part of your father. And that is the part that I refuse to live with."

I gasped, unable to keep the sobs at bay. "Let me go, Alex. I'll leave here remembering the man who saved my life and how he loved me more fiercely than anyone has before. I give you my word."

He stared at me with tears running down his face, and with a hopeful expression.

I continued, "You can do great things. You could change the lives of others, but you have to repair the brokenness inside of you before you can do it. Ask for forgiveness and change. Promise me. Promise me you'll get help."

He dropped the gun to the ground and placed both hands on my face. "Please don't leave me. Everyone leaves me. You're everything to me."

"Promise me, you will get help, Alex."

"I promise you, Liv, I promise. I love you so much." He fell to his knees in tears.

It was hard to watch a large, strong man like Alex crumble to the ground. I slowly backed up toward the dock, and when I had faith he wouldn't shoot me in the back, I took off running. I jumped in the boat with Mary, and she released the knot to our freedom.

The boat was about a hundred feet from the dock when he made eye contact with me, and doubt crept into my heart.

Are you doing the right thing?

He made mistakes, but I'd never find anyone that loved me as much as Alex did. Isabel said he would walk through fire for me. Would I ever find that again? I was confused and broken-hearted. Tormented by love and unforgiving pain piercing my chest.

Mary's gaze met mine, and I knew she could sense the struggle. "You have to listen to me." She grabbed my arm to keep my attention. "There's nothing back there for you. His demons are too great for you to live with. There isn't anything we can do to help him. He has to do that himself. You can go be the mother that Sophia needs. Okay? I need you to stay with me. I need you."

She was right. I couldn't stay with him, but my heart didn't understand that.

I sat in silence because I knew Mary was right. But Alex had a large piece of my heart, and that part of me just shattered on Isle Luciana. I didn't know if I would ever be the same. I had to focus on what mattered. I sat in the boat, curled in a ball, talking myself out of a breakdown.

What just happened? Guilt combined with sadness was a destructive combination for the soul. The deaths of two men haunted me, but I remembered the lives of the women they had ruined. Alex was a part of that, and I had to remind myself of that every time my heart felt like breaking.

16

I struggled to take in everything that happened when we arrived at San Brilee Island. Officers ran out to the dock when someone started screaming that our clothes were covered in blood. We were taken in for questioning, and a large man with a dark complexion and bald head came into the room.

"Ma'am? Can you hear me?"

I nodded slightly, but enough for him to notice.

"Can you tell me your name?"

I didn't answer immediately, so Mary responded.

"Mary Hernandez," she answered. The officer turned back toward me.

"And you?" he asked.

"Olivia. Olivia Brinkley, I managed to get out."

The officer leaned against his desk as if he needed the support. Rubbing his palms down his face, his expression looked tormented. "Jesus, Charlie, do you know who this is? We searched San Adler for her after a tip was called in recently."

"Yeah, I know who she is. Poor thing is in shock. Get on

the phone Murphy and get me someone from Homeland Security."

This got my attention, and I tried to snap out of my haze. It would have been so easy to let sorrow overtake me. But, people needed me. Sophia and Mary needed me, and they were just kids.

"I'm sorry? A tip?" I asked.

"Yes, ma'am. A couple of tourists called and said you were seen at the island market over on San Adler. We investigated, but the trail was cold."

Herb and his wife, bless them. They tried to help me.

"No one else ever called? After the report was filed?" I asked.

"Report? Ms. Brinkley, we never received a report. Your picture has been released on every major news station known to man. If a report was called in verifying your presence in our area, we would have been there." No report had ever been filed. Lie after lie piled up.

I looked to my left at Mary, older than her years, sitting like an unmovable force to be reckoned with. I couldn't believe how strong she had been through all of this. She must've known how torn my heart was, as she refused to leave my side.

The officers gave us a change of clothes and had their physician check us out for injuries. I overheard the doctor telling the men that the blood on our clothes wasn't ours, so the officers came in demanding answers. We told them everything from start to finish. They were shocked and appalled that this had gone on in their jurisdiction for so long without them knowing.

"Ma'am, if what you say is true. Then we haven't only failed you, but many others." He stared at me with a sad and disturbed expression.

I thought back to Alex's comment about the officers

being no better than mall security. That wasn't true. This operation was just too big and too hidden for these guys to uncover.

The men swiftly sent a crew to the island to check our story, and within a few hours, Charlie and Murphy came back into our holding cell. "Ladies, we'll get you two on a plane back to the states as soon as possible. Your family is being notified."

As the officers started to leave the room, I called out, "Excuse me."

"Yes?" Murphy asked.

"So, you found them?"

"Yes, ma'am, we did. Luciana was on the dock when we arrived. She showed us where the bodies were located and told us everything. You have a witness, so there isn't a reason to doubt your story."

"And Alex?"

"Long gone, ma'am." A painful pressure built in my chest at his words.

"Poor Luciana, I can't imagine the lonely life she's lived," Mary stated.

"That wasn't a life at all," I replied.

We slept in the holding cell overnight until a detective arrived the next morning. He led us to a private room where a blonde-headed woman with kind blue eyes waited for us.

"Hello, Olivia, Mary. I'm Agent Branton, an agent with FEAR, and I would like to ask you some questions if that is alright."

"I'm sorry, FEAR?" I asked.

"Yes, Ma'am. The Force for education, avoidance, and rescue. We assist victims and families from kidnapping and trafficking crimes."

I closed my eyes at those words; a reminder of what happened that day at the airport. Mary and I took a seat in front of her. She wanted the story from the beginning, and we did our best to remember every detail.

She asked Mary in-depth questions about the Reed house before I arrived, and Mary tried to answer each one thoroughly. She then turned toward me and smiled. "It's amazing how much Sophia resembles you."

My breath caught, and tears filled my eyes. My throat tightened as I tried to hold myself together.

"She and I have become good friends since your disappearance, Liv. She is quite a young lady, and you should be proud."

I dropped my head in my hands and broke down. Although these were things I already knew, hearing them in the present situation was precisely what my heart needed. "Is she . . . is she okay? Does she know how hard I'm trying to get home?"

"She does, and she is very proud of you. You know, I lost my only daughter to trafficking over ten years ago." She paused to take a breath and fought the tears that filled her eyes. "I have never been able to find her. I cope by helping other families, like mine, when they lose loved ones to this horrid crime. Sophia never gave up, you know. She said you would find a way to come back to her. And she was right."

The hope that her daughter would be able to fight her way back remained in her eyes and the thought of what that child might have gone through crushed me.

"We will be taking the first flight out tomorrow, ladies, and I'll escort you back to the states. Mary, we are currently working on your paperwork to enter the US, okay?"

"Tomorrow? Why not today?" I asked.

"We have things to finalize here considering two bodies were found last night. We will get you back as soon as possible, but we don't want it to look like we are rushing because you're guilty. Understand?"

"Yes, we understand."

"Just get some rest, and I'll take care of everything for you. I'm proud of you both."

* * *

SEATED on a plane between Mary and Agent Branton, I couldn't relax. My mind and body were exhausted. The flight offered little comfort for sleep. Who was I kidding? I couldn't sleep if I wanted to. Every time I closed my eyes, I saw two men slumped over lifeless, and I would never be able to forget it.

I took a man's life. Mary took a man's life, and she was just seventeen years old. This kind, gracious young woman had done more for me than she would ever know, and I will spend the rest of my life making sure she enjoys hers.

My thoughts drifted to Alex, and an ache settled in my chest. Doubt often crept in, and my mind wandered what was real and what was fake in our relationship. Even after all of the lies and the pain, I still remembered the protective, handsome, strong man that knew exactly what I needed before I did myself. That was real. Alex loved me, and there isn't a soul on this earth that could convince me otherwise.

We had been through hours of questioning and wrote detailed statements to investigate the Reed family, as well as William and Ian's involvement in other kidnappings. I would do whatever it took to bring other young women home or prevent this from happening to anyone else.

We were only fifteen minutes from landing, and my palms were sweating. Agent Branton reached over to hold my hand and offered me some comfort. "Take a deep breath, Olivia."

I breathed deeply to control the lump in my throat and the hot burning sensation in my nose. I was going to see

Sophia. I could barely remember her face. Of all my memories that had resurfaced, that was the one thing I couldn't seem to get a clear image of. It had been months since she had seen me, what would she think of me? Would she be ashamed that I fell into this trap?

I remembered having her when I had just turned eighteen. I was a young mom on my own, but I loved every minute of it. Sophia had recently turned sixteen years old. My sweet, funny, and smart baby girl was sixteen years old. The memory of Alex telling me Ian had tried to coerce her made my skin crawl. My girl was too smart for that. Too bright for them.

I was overwhelmed at the things I needed to do when I returned. Sophia needed some time with me, and I had no idea if I still had a job. Mary needed to get settled.

Breathe Liv, not everything has to be done today.

The aircraft jerked and skidded to a stop, and my grip clamped tighter on the woman beside me. My hands shook, and my stomach dropped.

"We will be with you the entire time, okay?"

I nodded and stood to exit the airplane.

"Sophia is in a private room with your mom, Liv. It may take some time for us to get there. You are a little bit of a news sensation at the moment. If you get overwhelmed, give me a sign, and I'll get you out of there."

As we exited the tunnel, news crews stood everywhere, with flashing lights and microphones in my face, begging for live interviews with the human trafficking victim that had arrived home. The loud, chaotic atmosphere was very confusing. They shouted questions at me, and I wasn't sure which way to turn. I turned to Agent Branton for guidance, and she immediately stepped in front of me and took charge.

"Excuse me! Back there, excuse me! Can I have your attention, please?"

"I'm sure you can understand the relief of being home, but Ms. Brinkley has been through quite an ordeal, and we would appreciate a little space. As soon as things calm down, you may contact me for interview requests. But, for now, can we please focus on reuniting her with her family?"

The news crews backed off, and some started packing up their equipment. Agent Branton was a force to be reckoned with. I had never seen so many reporters before, and I'd never witnessed them give up so easily. I kept hold of Mary, and Agent Branton led us to a private room down a hall away from the media.

"That was insane," I said.

"Yes, I'm sorry about that. I had hoped it would be more contained."

We entered the small conference room, and she shut the door behind us.

"Mom." A small voice from inside the room called out to me, and my chest tightened.

"Sophia." My beautiful dark-haired, brown-eyed baby girl stood staring at me. Those brown eyes that brought me so much comfort the first day I woke up lost and confused.

She bolted across the room, and we collided, holding each other in the middle of the floor. This was my reason. This was why I fought so hard. At the end of the day, it was all about getting back to her. I held her until the sobs left her little body. I held her until she knew I was really home, and I was not going anywhere. Another set of arms wrapped around us, and I looked up to see my mom sobbing over us.

"Oh, Livi," she cried. We sat together until the cracks in our hearts started to mend as if some higher power had begun stitching up the busted seams.

EPILOGUE

"Where is she?" I turned in my seat and stretched my neck to look for any sign of her. She was already supposed to be there, and it was going to start at any moment. My feet tapped, and my hands fidgeted.

"Excuse me. Excuse me, ma'am. Pardon me." Mary's voice echoed from the end of the row.

"Thank God you made it," I exclaimed. "She would kill you if you hadn't."

"Are you kidding? I would not miss this for the world," she said, beaming.

I looked toward the other side of my seat where Mom and Agent Branton sat. "You two look as nervous as I am," I told them.

"I think we are," Mom admitted with the utmost seriousness.

Since I disappeared over two years ago, Sophia and Agent Branton had forged a bond as thick as family. The closeness had only bloomed since my return, and I was grateful to call her part of our clan. Mary had also made strides since she had been with us. The first year, Sophia prepared Mary for her GED. She passed with flying colors and immediately started college courses online.

After a few semesters, she became more confident and took classes with other students. She had already earned a scholarship for her last two years of college and secured an internship at the publishing company I worked for. When I returned, I received a promotion with more benefits. When my boss told me I wouldn't have to travel anymore, I accepted. I'm good at staying in the states for a while.

Mary was lively, vibrant, and happier than she had ever been. I kept telling her she would have her own publishing company one day, and I'd come work for her. Mary just shook her head and laughed. She and Sophia had become as close as sisters.

A few months after we returned from the island, Mary received a visit from an attorney, Alex's attorney. I watched her sweet face fall apart when she found out who her true father was and what he did to her mother. I had been struggling with the decision on when I should tell her, and I hated that it came from his lawyer.

He explained to Mary that Alex no longer wanted anything to do with the Reed Corporation. He had already placed a percentage of the money into an account for Luciana. The rest would be left to Mary. She would have to return to the island to finalize details with the estate when she was ready. She sat numb, listening to the strange, emotionless man, then he got up to leave.

"Do you know where he is? Alex?"

"No ma'am. From my understanding, no one does." He left without another word.

Mary opened a folder and pulled out a thick pile of paperwork. Two small envelopes fell out; one addressed to Mary and one to myself. Mary opened hers first and read it aloud while I took in every word, as if I could hear his voice.

Mary,

I know I haven't always done right by you, and this is me saying I'm sorry. Nothing that happened between my father and your mother was your fault, and I shouldn't have blamed you. Please forgive me and accept what is rightfully yours.

Alex

Mary lowered the letter with tears in her eyes and smiled. "I have a brother. I've always wanted a sibling. I mean, he's a complicated brother, but he's still better than my father."

We both started laughing at that absurd truth. Bless that girl's heart, she still looked for the silver lining in all of this.

That night before bed, I pulled out the envelope with my name on it. I'd been too much of a coward all day to read it. Tears ran down my face at his words, and there was nothing I wanted more than to be held by him right then.

Liv,

I hope you know I will never stop trying to right my wrongs. You made me the best version of myself, and I want to thank you for that.

Forever yours,

Alex

* * *

AROUND 6 MONTHS after receiving Alex's letter, Mary returned to San Adler to tie up loose ends. I offered to go with her, but Mary said she knew it would be too difficult for me. Agent Branton escorted her so she wouldn't be alone. Mary decided to sell Reed Pharmaceuticals. There was too much corrupt history and horrid former exploits in the company for her to have anything to do with it. She used very little money to get started with clothing and supplies, then invested some to have on hand in case it was needed for college costs.

While in San Adler, Mary visited Luciana. We had been concerned about her since Alex disappeared and wanted to make sure she was okay.

"Did she look well? Does she need anything?" I asked Mary on her return.

"She looked as lovely as ever. She seems to have everything she needs," she said with a sly grin.

"What does that mean?" I asked.

"Well, do you remember officer Murphy?" Mary grinned and wagged her eyebrows.

"No! Are you serious?"

"Very serious. Luciana seemed somewhat pleased with herself about it. She declined flying out to visit, but does request that you write to her and send lots of pictures."

"And Isabel?"

"She, um, she isn't doing as well. She's not only carrying a lot of guilt for what her husband did, but she is also grieving him. There are no hard feelings toward you or me, but she does need some time to process everything. She seems lonely, and now that the house is closed, she doesn't have anything to keep her mind occupied. So, I decided to keep the house open and make Isabel house manager," she admitted.

"You what? Are you sure that's what you want?" Keeping the house open would tie Mary to the island. I wasn't sure she had thought it through.

"Yes, Isabel will do an excellent job, and we're going to open the house as a bed and breakfast. That way, everyone will be able to keep their employment, and it may bring some tourists to the island. Plus, I don't have to travel back there to maintain the house. Isabel is going to communicate with my financial advisor for everything."

I was impressed. This sweet young girl had a knack for business and compassion for people in need. I was in awe of her strength and endurance more and more every day.

"It sounds like everything went well while you were there," I said.

"Well, almost," she said, chewing the side of her cheek.

"What happened?"

"Anna and Miguel caught up with me on the dock as I was leaving." The pain on her face told me more than I needed to know. "They are just hurting, Liv. They want to blame someone for Alex leaving, and we are easy targets. They never liked me anyway. But, now I realize it's because they knew Richard Reed was my father."

"I know you're right. I just hate they are suffering."

"Me too. At least I have the house situated, and I want you to know that half of the profits have been put into an account for the baby. I want my nephew to be taken care of once he is born," she told me with tears in her eyes.

"Also, I'm keeping the sailboat for him. I want him to have something of his father's, something that is special to both of you."

* * *

I LOOKED DOWN at the beautiful chubby dark-haired toddler in my lap. The amount of love this family held for this child was more than he could ever need. Such an innocent in all of this disarray. Sophia asked me what I would tell him about his father, and my answer was simple.

"Your father saved my life, and I fell in love with him."

This baby was conceived out of love, and that's all he needed to know.

When I found out I was pregnant, I cried. I cried for weeks. Trapped between sadness that this part of my life would never be over and happiness that this miracle would shed light on a dark time. I even talked to Luciana over the phone about trying to inform Alex about the baby, but she declined to help. Whether she didn't know how to find him or didn't think I should, I wasn't sure.

"Move on with your life, and don't look back sweet Liv."

The thought of having a constant reminder of what I'd lost with Alex tore my heart to shreds. But, when he was born, and I saw the greatest parts of Alex staring back at me with adoring eyes, I fell in love all over again.

"Come on, Archer. Come to Aunt Mary," she said as she reached out for him. "That's my sweet boy!"

She peppered kisses all over his chubby neck, and he giggled as his bright green eyes shone up at me. This was the best part of Alex, the greatest gift he could have given me. My chest still ached, but my heart was full. I fingered the necklace around my throat. The combination of Sophia's gold plate and the teardrop diamond was a reminder of what I had been through, and what my future held. I never wanted to forget.

"It's starting," Mary said.

One by one, the graduates lined the stage, and we all cried and cheered as Sophia crossed the platform to receive her diploma. All four of us sniffled and handed out tissues. It was when I looked at the graduation program that I couldn't contain my emotions any longer.

SOPHIA RAE BRINKLEY

"After my internship with Agent Branton and Homeland Security, my goal is to become an Undercover Recovery Agent with FEAR to assist the victims of human trafficking."

. . .

I LOOKED over at Agent Branton, and tears rolled down her face. "She wanted to surprise you. She's focused and determined, Liv. She will make you proud," she said.

"I have no doubt." I didn't think I could be more proud.

So much was to be learned from my experience, and one day I hoped to have the courage and strength to tell my story to millions of people. Not only women, but small children were ripped from their homes daily, never to return. Until I could be the courageous voice I wanted to be, I knew my family would be by my side, fighting that fight alongside me.

My greatest hope was that my situation would draw awareness to human trafficking and bring victims home to their families. Home to heal the wounds this evil world had created.

And maybe, just maybe one day my heart would finally heal. As I gazed into my child's beautiful green eyes, I heard his father's words echoing in my head, as strong as the day we met.

"You can trust me."

I could only hope and pray that someday my heart wouldn't break from the memory.

BROKEN TRUST, BOOK TWO

NOW AVAILABLE

ABOUT THE AUTHOR

A.F. Presson's career in writing began in 2021 with a women's fiction novel titled Blind Trust, soon followed by Broken Trust and Interference. Blind Trust was awarded Distinguished Favorite in Women's Fiction from the Independent Press Awards and also a finalist for the Annie McDonnell Book Award.

Amanda, born in Chattanooga, TN, resides in North Alabama with her husband Brian, and their two sons, Roman and Isaac. When she isn't writing, she is working in a local electrophysiology lab and spending time with her family. An avid fan of music and Broadway, the arts have always played a large part in her life and she embraces the opportunity to enter the world of literature.

ALSO BY A.F. PRESSON

Women's Fiction

Blind Trust: The Trust Series Book One

Broken Trust: The Trust Series Book Two

Fragile Trust: (Coming Soon!)

Young Adult Fantasy

Interference: Book One

Oblivion: Book Two (Coming Soon!)

Inspirational

Chronicles of a Lost Boy on Christmas